Waiting on Forever

SWEET NOTHINGS BAKE SHOP, BOOK 3

KRISTEN DIXON

THIGPEN-GANDY PUBLISHING

Contents

Dedication   V

1. PTA   1

2. Mayhem & Mornings   14

3. Field Trips & Foibles   28

4. The Check Out   40

5. Not a Date   52

6. Lawyer Friend   69

7. House Shopping   80

8. Legally Broke   91

9. Hercules   99

10. In The Attic   109

11. Furry Bandit   118

12. Charitable   131

13. Crisis Mode   144

14. The Big D   153

15. Ice Cream and Expectations   174

16. Official   186

17. Wise Council   207

18. Spring Extravaganza   216

19. Dancing in the Moonlight   228

20. Epilogue   236

Before You Go . . .   242

Also By Kristen Dixon   244

About the Author   247

For Jojo.

Your spirit could not be tamed, and your laughter lit every room you were in.

Cancer may have won the fight, but the impact you left on my life has never diminished, and I will always miss you.

ONE

PTA

Waiting tables was a hectic business. I'd been to my share of crowded restaurants, but never on this side of the equation before. Usually, I was the frazzled mom trying to keep Josie from chucking her toy into the aisle where someone would break their neck. Now, I was the frazzled waitress trying to balance twelve very full sweet teas on a tray, while crossing the busy restaurant to the table where the school PTA was having their monthly meeting. *Don't drop it, Maggie, you can do this!*

I successfully navigated the chaos, and painstakingly got the lip of the tray onto the table where I slid it to safety. *Phew.* "Okay, everyone ... sweet teas all around, and then I can take your orders if you're ready." I smiled and began passing out the drinks.

A blonde woman at the end laughed. "No rush—Lacy's never going to make her mind up in the next ten minutes." The brunette to her right smacked her arm indignantly but didn't argue.

"Well, take your time. It's no trouble at all," I assured them as I quickly left the table before they changed their minds and tried to suck me into a conversation. A few minutes' break would be heaven. It was my first day working at Jude's, and I was feeling woefully out of shape already. You'd think running after my six-year-old daughter would have prepared me for this, but I was still dragging. I grabbed a fresh glass, scooped some ice out of the icemaker in the back, and poured myself a big glass of sweet tea. The first sip was heaven, and I propped my hip against the counter where I could still keep an eye on my first-ever big table.

My gaze roamed the restaurant—just starting to fill up with the lunch rush—and then wandered out to the parking lot. This little town was pretty predictable, unlike where Josie and I used to live. But something about the pickups and family sedans was oddly soothing, as if nothing bad could happen in a place with such sedate cars. A white truck with state park decals on it pulled up and caught my attention, breaking the monotony.

Someone from the park service must be coming in for lunch. I wonder if they're local, or just passing through?

A tall, brunette man in a park ranger's uniform stepped out of the truck, and I almost stopped breathing. He was absolutely the most stunning male specimen I'd ever seen. Chiseled jaw, thick hair poking out from underneath a ball cap, five o'clock shadow—and that uniform clung to his biceps in an enticing manner. He was rapidly approaching the front door of the restaurant, and I snapped my eyes back over to my large table, away from his danger-ously handsome face. *He is way out of your league, and not at all what you should be worried about right now, Maggie. You're soon-to-be divorced and have a six-year-old. That Adonis isn't in the market for your hot mess.*

Shaking off the instant attraction, I set my tea back down and crossed to my large table to take their order. I managed to get all twelve orders cap-tured accurately and into the kitchen window be-fore sneaking another glance around the restaurant for the intriguing park ranger. I spotted him in Ash-ley's section, right next to mine. His head was down, still browsing the menu.

He must not be from here, because just about everyone who came in the door had the menu memorized and a usual Tuesday order. Sue buzzed past and pulled me from my woolgathering.

"Mags, can you roll some more silverware? I'm slammed, people are pouring in, and we're already on the last bucket. Breakfast shift was *slacking*." She shot a pointed look at Ashley, who just shook her head and silently scooted past to the window.

"Sure, of course." I hustled over to the silverware station and started rolling. It was a mindless task, but the only extra thing they'd trained me to do this morning besides the basic table waiting skills I already had from high school. I had an impressive stack in a new bucket by the time my order was called, and I'd only peeked at Mr. Gorgeous approximately eighty-seven times along the way. He was studiously reading a handbook with a green cover and hadn't noticed my attention.

"Order up, Maggie!" Anthony called behind me, and I turned to see him shoving plates in the window as fast as he could, and Denise was right behind him holding more.

"Coming!" I snatched up a tray and loaded up the first round to deliver to the PTA. I started with blondie at the end since she seemed most likely to talk my ear off if I didn't feed her quickly enough.

It took four trips to get all the plates delivered, and then an extra for condiments and napkins, before I headed back to the silverware station to keep a watchful eye out for drinks getting low.

The stack continued to grow at an impressive rate when Ashley interrupted. "Hey, Maggie, I know they've got you only working on the big table since it's your first day, but do you think you could handle one more? My shift ended fifteen minutes ago, and Sue is mad at me and won't take my new table. It's just one guy, and I already put his ticket in the window, so it should be easy money." She pointed her thumb over her shoulder at the table where Mr. Handsome was seated.

"Oh, uhm—"

"Thanks, you're a gem!" Ashley cut me off and waved her apron at me in thanks as she bolted for the back door.

"Sure, I'd love to take your table, Ashley." I muttered. Before I could overthink it, someone from my PTA table waved a near-empty tea glass at me, so I scooped up a pitcher and headed over.

After I finished up their drinks, Mr. Handsome's club with fries was already in the window, so I grabbed that and hurried across the room to deliver it.

"Hi. Club sandwich?" I asked, all business.

He blinked and flipped his book closed with one hand as he looked up at me with a wry grin. "Most people call me Jensen, but"—he looked me up and down in one smooth motion—"sure, you can call me anything you want."

My jaw dropped at the obvious flirtation, but a little frisson of heat suffused my skin regardless. *Was this guy serious?* "Uh, right . . . well, here's your lunch." I picked my jaw up and sat the plate in front of him, as his eyes twinkled with humor. Gorgeous, sparkling green eyes, like I'd never seen before. I pointedly looked away and noticed his glass was empty. "Can I get you a refill? What are you having?" *There, a good safe topic.*

He grabbed the cup and passed it over. "Water, thanks."

I took the glass with a nod and filled it from the pitcher behind the counter. While I was at it, I took a few deep breaths to calm my suddenly rampant heartbeat and snuck another peek at him over the counter. He was just sitting there enjoying his sandwich and taking in the restaurant. He didn't look like a raging flirt, although he certainly had the looks to get away with it. Most women would probably eat it up.

Most women weren't coming out of a manure-pile of a relationship where the S-O-B left them for a nineteen-year-old "model," either. Right. And he wouldn't be interested in me, regardless. Too old—as Carl had told me—and way too much baggage. Now fortified with a bracing dose of reality, I carried his water back to him, with my boss Janie's voice floating in my memory the whole way.

Here's the secret to small-town waitressing, Magnolia: People don't mind a slower pace, but you've got to kill them with kindness. Food's wrong? Keep smiling and make it right. Somebody's been waiting on their no-good uncle for half an hour and they're crabby? Smile harder, keep the drinks full, and bring them an appetizer on the house. They'll appreciate the effort. No matter what comes up, your attitude is going to make all the difference. People won't forget your kindness.

I forced a polite smile as I approached Mr. Handsome's—excuse me, *Jensen's*—table. "Here you go. Can I get you anything else to go with that—ketchup, napkins . . .?"

A slow smile crept across his face, the action driving a shiver down my spine. "Naw, darlin', that'll be fine for now."

Heat crept at my neck at his calling me darlin', but I just smiled and reminded myself that the seventy-eight-year-old man in the parking lot had called me the same thing this morning.

I ducked away and turned on my heel to go check on the PTA table again.

"—I'm telling you, Frank, it's a bad idea. I don't care how trendy it is to encourage spray paint art now—it's not safe for kids to use spray paint. The fumes are bad, end of discussion," a severe-looking man at the end of the table insisted.

Blondie chimed in, "Not to mention it would really backfire on us when they hit the teen years. Every bridge in the tri-county area is going to get tagged, and who wants to pay to clean that up?" She shook her head dryly and stabbed a crouton with her fork.

I quietly collected the one or two empty plates so far and left them to their arguments. Safely back behind the bar, I checked on Jensen again. There he was, nose buried back in the handbook, contentedly chewing his sandwich. I replayed the moment of him smiling and calling me darlin' about twelve times, imagining how different my life would be if I'd lived in Adele and met Jensen, instead of my almost-ex-husband. The park ranger's uniform clung to his upper chest and arms distractingly as he took the next bite of his sandwich, and I forced myself to look down at the silverware bucket, and resumed wrapping. Hands no longer idle, I drifted into the fantasy of a wholesome and heat-filled life if it had started with McHunk over there, instead of Carl.

Small-town sweethearts, we'd have had eyes only for each other. He'd have taken me to prom, where we'd dance the night away. Then it would have ended with a stolen kiss on the porch swing before my dad turned the lights on and caught us. He'd have proposed a year later, on one knee by the river, with a tiny perfect diamond, and love in his eyes. We'd have worked hard, him training as an entry level ranger, me working right here at the restaurant until Josie came along, tiny and pink and perfect to complete the picture. Sure, we'd fight over dumb little things like who forgot to wash the socks, but in the end we'd make up and sneak into the kitchen for a slice of chocolate cake at midnight. I sighed, the image almost painfully perfect, compared to the reality I'd had with Carl.

He'd been so appealing at first. All suave, slicked back hairstyle, and well-dressed flair. He drove a nice car and took me to nice restaurants. He had so much ambition.

All I'd seen was the surface—his shine, and the way he always knew what to say. But then he'd spent the first years of our marriage trotting me about like eye candy to his co-workers. There only to impress, not to cherish. Ten years and a pregnancy later, the shine had worn off, and he'd wandered along to the next naive young thing . . . and left me to reside on my aunt's couch. What I hadn't realized in my naivete was that ambition had made him cold. The divorce wasn't a surprise, now that I had my eyes open to the truth of him, and had some time away from him to think about it.

I scanned the PTA table, and saw them finishing up, so I abandoned my mountain of silverware and fruitless daydreams to prep their individual checks so I could drop them off with another round of sweet teas. Janie had instructed me before they walked in—they'd eat first, and then I'd just keep them topped off with tea while they finished their meeting. They'd leave me a healthy tip for my first day, and I could learn the menu and the ropes. I walked back over to Jensen's table, and he'd pushed his empty plate aside, absorbed right back into his manual.

"How was everything?" I asked softly, and he looked startled as he glanced up at me. "Sorry, I didn't mean to scare you. That must be a good book."

"Oh, just a work thing. I'm trying to brush up on a new conservation project we're starting." He set it aside and scorched me with another of those wide smiles of his. "Everything was great, thank you."

"I'm glad to hear it. Would you like a water for the road?"

He flung a hand to his chest, as if wounded. "In such a hurry to get rid of me already?"

I drew my eyebrows up in surprise. "Oh, no, of course not—Janie told me that most of the lunch crowd who come in uniform appreciate things moving quickly, so they can get back to work. You can stay as long as you want, I—"

He lifted a hand and rested it gently on my forearm, effectively cutting off my ramble with a pleasurable zing. "Hey, I was joking. You're doing just fine, and I do need to get back on the road. Thank you for being considerate." His tone was so sincere, and my eyes got trapped in his forest-green gaze.

"Sorry, it's my first day," I mumbled, embarrassed at not catching his sarcasm.

His smile was slow this time, spreading like the morning sun on a damp field. "Does that mean I'll be seeing you around?"

"Uhm, I guess so. If you're not just passing through."

He chuckled. "Let's just say I pass through a lot."

"Then, yes, I guess." *Why do I sound so unsure of myself? He is putting me off-balance without even trying.*

He dug into his pocket for his wallet, pulled out a twenty, and passed it to me. "Keep the change."

I quickly did the math in my head, and his sandwich hadn't cost nearly enough to use up a twenty; he was leaving me a hundred percent tip. "You really don't have to; I was only here a few minutes. This is too much."

He shook his head at my protest. "You aren't supposed to argue when someone tries to tip you. That's the whole point of waitressing, right?"

I blinked at him, unable to argue with that logic. I shouldn't be arguing with anything that helped me put food on the table for Josie, and eventually got us out of Aunt Celia's hair. "Well, I'll just say thank you, then."

"You're welcome . . . ?"

"Oh, sorry, I forgot I don't have a name tag yet. Maggie. Well, Magnolia, but everyone just calls me Maggie." I snapped my mouth closed to stop any more rambling from spewing out.

"Magnolia," he said my name slowly, rolling it over his tongue with a precise drawl. "Beautiful." He met my eyes as he said it, and I couldn't tell if he meant the name, or me. Heat bloomed in my stomach, and I stepped nervously away. "Thank you again, Jensen."

"It was a pleasure, Magnolia." He nodded and then strode out of the restaurant, waving at people he knew on the way out.

I crossed to the register to cash him out but couldn't seem to concentrate until after I'd watched him back the big white truck out and pull out of the lot. Once it was completely out of sight, the fog cleared, and I punched in the ticket details. By that time, Sue was waiting rather impatiently to handle one of her own tickets.

"Sorry," I mumbled and rushed to step out of her way, nearly taking out an umbrella stand in the process. *Smooth, Maggie. Gawk, moon-eyed, at the first handsome man who waltzes through and perturb your coworkers while you're at it. Real smooth.*

I hustled across the floor back to my safe space behind the silverware bucket. The PTA wasn't anywhere near done with their meeting by the looks of the raised hands and rolling eyes, so I had a while to settle in, and ponder the feelings coursing through me—the ones I desperately wanted to deny signified attraction. Intense, unexpected attraction.

TWO

Mayhem & Mornings

The foghorn blaring of my cell phone alarm peeled my eyelids open before the sun was awake the next morning, and reality felt like a mule kick to the teeth. I slapped out a hand to silence the raging cruise ship, and then rubbed my gritty eyelids. How could I be so tired all afternoon, and then lie down at night to stare at the ceiling until one-thirty a.m.? It made no sense, but my freaking alarm didn't care. I rolled to my back, and stared at the ceiling, questioning all of my life choices there in the dark. *How did I get here? I thought my life was on track. Stay-at-home mom to a beautiful and brilliant daughter, successful husband, loving family . . .* then, crash. One minute I was on top of the world, the next I was at the bottom of the heap. Right that minute I felt every bump and bruise on the way down, all the way to my soul.

The cursed alarm began to wail again, and with a sigh I rolled over and turned it off. With nothing but sheer, dogged determination, I pulled myself through my morning routine, and then went in to wake Josie.

"Baby girl," I whispered, "it's time to get up for school."

She didn't respond, just huffed a little in her sleep. Her pajama shirt was pulled up, showing off her little belly pooch, and I watched her breathe for a minute, soaking in the quiet peace of her. Settling on the edge of the bed, I tried again.

"Josie, come on now—open those eyes. We have to get to school today."

"School?" She rubbed her eyes but didn't open them. Instead, she flipped to her belly, poking her butt into the air.

"Don't try to get back to sleep. Come on, up!" I demanded and shimmied the covers off her.

"Mo-o-om . . ." She snatched her pillow over her tangled mess of curls, and I couldn't help but grin. *She gets that from me.*

"Jo-o-o-sie. If you get up right now, I'll make you special pancakes." I waited, knowing she'd take the bait.

Her elbow wiggled under the edge of the pillow, and I knew she was on the hook. A moment later, she mumbled, "Special pancakes?"

"*Special* pancakes. You can choose chocolate chips or sprinkles. What are you in the mood for today?"

She didn't move the pillow, just sat upright and let it flop to the side. "I want both. Bye, Mom!" In two seconds flat, she had swung her legs over the edge of the bed and was tottering off to the bathroom.

I shook my head but made my way to the kitchen for double-special pancake-making. I didn't do it every day, but it was her first day at the new school, and I wanted to make sure she knew that we hadn't changed, even though everything around us had. It nagged at me, the worry that I was going to screw things up for her. It was so much pressure, feeling the need to be everything for her. *Apparently when Carl left, he left all the worries that should be his with me, too.*

Forcing myself to shake off thoughts of my bastard ex, I grabbed a box of pancake mix and started mixing. I was just pouring the first one on the pan when Aunt Celia walked in.

"Maggie, my girl, what are you doing cooking at this hour?" she admonished.

"Making pancakes?"

"Honey, the sun ain't even made an appearance and there is batter on the floor. I know you're Supermom; you don't have to do everything yourself to prove it." She slid a carafe of orange juice from the fridge and eyed me over the rim of her tortoiseshell glasses.

"I'm nothing close to Supermom . . . I just want her to have a great first day." I flipped the pancake, tears misting my eyes, again. *When did I become such a crier?* Oh, somewhere between the, "I found a new woman," and the, "Have a nice life . . . somewhere else." I shook it off and checked the spot Celia had pointed out. "And I will clean the floor, sorry."

She smiled at me as she pulled a glass from the cabinet and pressed a kiss to my cheek. "Well, I can't fault you for wanting to start her off on a good foot today. But, you're going to have to let me finish up for you, or you'll be late, and definitely don't worry about the floor. It'll keep."

"Who's gonna be late? Am I? I don't want to be late, or no one will play with me at recess. They already don't know who I am!" Josie came stumbling into the kitchen, half of her hair sticking straight up still, and a look of pure panic on her face as she scrambled

17

onto a barstool. Her fear made my heart squeeze, and I felt tears prickle at the back of my eyes.

Celia looked up from her coffee mug, already half-drained. "Baby girl, don't you worry about a thing. Aunt Celia's going to take you to school, and we will be early so I can walk you in. Did you know I knew your teacher? I baked her sister's wedding cake four years ago!" Celia crossed the kitchen, and steered Josie by the shoulders back to her room for a good hair brushing, if I had to guess.

I was sliding the first two pancakes onto Josie's plate as Celia called down the hall, "Leave the pancakes on the counter and get to work! We'll be just fine."

With a sigh, I dropped the plate next to the mixing bowl and snatched up my keys. "I love you, baby! Have a great first day!" I was almost to the front door when I was nearly tackled by a waist-high hug.

"Love you too, Mama. I'm going to miss you."

The sadness in her voice nearly ripped me in half. My sweet, vibrant girl had never been the least bit shy of school before. Now I had to pull her away from her kindergarten friends in the middle of the year, to a new town, in a new house . . . and completely turn her world upside down. A tiny voice in the back of my head whispered that I hadn't asked Carl to cheat, but I shut it out. I had to focus on the here and now if I was going to make it through. One foot in front of the other; repeat daily until I got somewhere.

I sunk down to a crouch, so I could be eye to eye with her. "Hey, what do we say?" I asked, giving her upper arms a reassuring squeeze.

"Be kind to others and they will be kind to you," she recited dutifully.

"That's right. And you are the kindest, smartest, most beautiful person I know, inside and out. So even though you're new, they are going to see that and want to play with you and make friends."

She bit her tiny lip, before asking, "Promise?"

"Promise. Besides, Mrs. Levi owes Aunt Celia a favor, remember?"

"I remember," she grumbled.

"Okay then, nobody disappoints Aunt Celia. Including us," I added with a whisper. With one last kiss on her cheek, I ran out the door, tossing a prayer up on the way for the kids at Josie's school to be in an embracing sort of mood.

As soon as I was on my way, I dialed up my divorce mediator. A rotten way to start a Wednesday morning, but it was a fact of life right now. She answered on the second ring.

"This is Rose." Her voice was oddly chipper for someone in her profession.

"Hi, Rose, It's Maggie Abbott. I was just wondering if Mr. Abbott has responded to the initial papers you sent over? I don't want to be in limbo any longer than we have to."

"I totally understand, Mrs. Abbott. We'll follow up with him if we haven't heard anything by Thursday or Friday."

I sighed. "Thank you. And please, call me Maggie."

"Sure thing, Maggie."

I hung up and resisted the urge to let my head drop to the steering wheel while driving. Carl had promised he'd make things efficient and polite for Josie's sake. Now that we'd moved out like he wanted—crickets. It was infuriating, but I didn't have the money to find a lawyer. He had one, but all I'd asked for was basic child support and my half of our joint finances. Nothing crazy, so I didn't understand the sudden hold up. *He* was the one who'd abruptly decided to end things. I smacked the steering wheel, but I may have pretended it was his smug face.

My first full shift at the restaurant was incredibly hectic, but despite it all I spent the whole day peeking out the window for my favorite park ranger and wondering what new project he was working on. Stupid, maybe, but true. Today, I kept double-taking at every brunette man of roughly the right age, which had earned me some funny looks. It was a small town, but surely I couldn't be the quirkiest person here.

It was the tail-end of my shift, and I was dead on my feet and bussing a booth in the back corner of the restaurant, when a rumbly masculine voice came from my left.

"Is this seat taken? I'm told it's the only one available in your section." Jensen's words sent a flood of warmth to my cheeks as I stood bolt upright, startled by his sudden appearance.

"Jensen! Of course, have a seat."

His smile was brighter than the sun on a cloudless day. "You remember me?"

I tucked a curly black lock behind my ear before answering, "Of course. Why shouldn't I?"

"Oh, you definitely should remember me." He waggled his eyebrows, and I shook my head at his exaggerated silliness. How old was this guy? He looked my age. "I certainly remember you." His voice dropped even lower, and I swallowed hard, feeling suddenly hot.

"Well, what can I get you today? My shift is almost over, but I can at least start your order for you." I whipped out my ordering pad, intent on getting the conversation to safe ground.

He wasn't having it. "I'll take Granny's famous tea today, and have you had lunch yet?"

"Do you want sweet or unsweet?"

He chortled. "You really are new here. Granny's famous tea only comes in sweet. Also, you didn't answer my question."

"Uh, well, no . . . I haven't," I admitted.

"Great, you can sit and keep me company." He must have seen my shock clear as day because he hurried to add, "If you want, I mean. You don't *have* to; I can take no for an answer. But I'd love to talk to you some more." His smile faltered, and I answered on impulse.

"Sure, I'll sit with you. Let me put our orders in and I'll clock out." I spun to walk away, and then spun right back. "I am going to need your order to do that, though." I grimaced, hating that I felt so discombobulated by him. Not as much as I hated *showing* it to him, though.

"Club sandwich and fries, please."

"Coming right up." This time when I spun, I crossed quickly to the window, shoved in the ticket, and asked Denise to make me a club and fries, too. It sounded good.

By the time I'd finished hanging up my apron, clocking out with Janie—who promised to tally my credit card tips for me—and grabbed two sweet teas, the sandwiches were done.

I carried it all over on a tray and unloaded it to the table where he was waiting patiently, nose buried in his handbook again. He tucked it onto the bench next to him, and I made a mental note to ask him about his new project.

When I sat down across from him, a flutter of nerves assaulted me. What was I doing? I was still a married woman, and this was a small town. The rumor mill would have us eloping to the courthouse by the time dinner rolled around. I tucked my hands into my lap and then realized I couldn't eat that way, so picked up a fry and nibbled the end.

He seemed cool as a cucumber and took a huge bite of his club. After he swallowed he said, "Thank you, this is delicious."

"I didn't make it, but I'll tell Denise. She'll appreciate it. Most people take food for granted, since it's so easy to order out. It's a lot of work, back in the kitchen. And it's hot, you know, from all the stoves."

I tucked a wayward curl behind my ear, and bit my lip to stop the rambling.

He nodded, seeming amused by my word vomit. Which was good because he kept dragging ridiculous things out of my mouth. "So, busy day today?"

"Yeah, we were pretty slammed for breakfast, and lunch was hopping, too."

He nodded. "I usually come in for late lunch on weekdays if I'm in the area. Jude's is always slammed."

I picked up my sandwich and took a bite, the crispy bacon making me want to moan with pleasure. Breakfast had been far too long ago, and I was suddenly famished. "So, you come here a lot?"

He shrugged and nodded. "It's the best place to eat in Adele, for sure. But sometimes I'm on the other side of the park and can't get away. I usually brown bag it if I know I won't be close."

"Which park do you work at?"

"Oh, over at the Savannah Wildlife Refuge. It's a huge park, but there's a branch of it near here."

"That's awesome. What is this new project you're working on?" I waved at the handbook he'd been studying.

"It's top secret, but for you I'll make an exception."

Now it was my turn to bust out a laugh, and I watched, mortified, as sandwich crumbs sprayed out from between my lips onto the table. I clapped a hand over my face, sure I was turning beet red. "Oh my gosh."

"Don't be embarrassed, it was cute." He reached over and grabbed my wrist, tugging gently to get me to uncover my face. He swirled his fingertips over the inside of my wrist before he released me and launched into enthusiastically telling me about his project.

"There's been a project in recent years on private land, where volunteer companies create new wetland habitats to help support waterfowl, after their natural habitats have been destroyed. We're trying to expand that concept and build a new wetland habitat to support a local duck species which is in trouble. If we can successfully convert this new land into a workable habitat, it can be protected, and they can be supported. Hopefully start repopulating several native species, right here outside of Adele."

"Wow, that sounds like a really worthwhile project." I finally looked back down at my plate, only to realize I'd been so engrossed in his story that I'd polished off half my sandwich and most of the fries. I was stuffed. I looked over at his plate and he'd downed the whole thing.

"It is. It's important to protect the area's biodiversity, and those ducks make a bigger difference than people realize." He shot me another genuine smile, and then glanced down. "Shoot! I'm late. I hate to eat and run, especially when we've really just started getting to know each other . . . Would you like to go to dinner some time? Continue the conversation?"

He looked at me expectantly, and my heart nearly froze in my chest. I could not go on a *date* with him. I was still married, legally. Sure, only *technically* at this point, until the divorce was final, but . . . I just couldn't. Sitting down at lunch didn't feel the same, not like a date.

He didn't wait for an answer, seeing my hesitation. "Dang, I screwed it up already. Was it the ducks? I talked too much. I'm sorry. Maybe another time." He grimaced and pulled out his wallet to pay for lunch.

"No!" I reached forward and grabbed his hand. "No, it's not you. I loved hearing about the ducks, and your project. It was fascinating, and I'd love to hear more, next time you come in. It's . . . my life is really complicated right now. I'm just getting out of a relationship, and—"

"Hey, it's okay," he said, eyes kind as they met mine. "You don't owe me an explanation, but I do appreciate it. Would you consider a coffee some time, maybe tell me about all these complications? I'm a really good listener, when I don't have a rapt audience for my duck project speech." A charming twinkle came back to his eye, and I could feel myself pulled to him like a magnet.

"Mmm . . ." I wavered, tempted even though I should *not* be with my life still so unsettled.

"Don't say no. There's just something about you, Magnolia . . . I've got to see you again. We'll talk next time I come in." He shot me a wink, laid thirty dollars on the table, and jogged towards the exit to make it back to work on time.

I watched him leave, my belly swarming with butterflies that I hadn't felt in a long, long time.

THREE

Field Trips & Foibles

T hursday and Friday were my days off this week, and after school drop-off I spent all day Thursday looking at online real estate listings, and making an exhaustive list of pros and cons. There wasn't much in my price range, and even less that looked cheerful and perfect to raise a six-year-old. By the end of the day, I had a meager list of prospects, and Celia's promise that she'd call her realtor friend the next day to show me the ones on my list. It was impossible not to notice the slight frown on her face as she read to the end.

When Friday rolled around, I was happy to have that onerous task done, so I could focus on Josie for the day. She'd made two friends, Lindsay and

Sherise, at school, and I was beyond grateful. She'd come home perked up and chattering about them on Wednesday, her usual self. Today, I'd get to meet them on the school field trip. I wouldn't be able to go on all of her school outings, but I was happy I could make this one. Changing schools mid-year was hard, and I wanted to do everything in my power to make things easier on her.

As I drove us to the school, I realized that I didn't actually know where we were going on the field trip. We'd missed the advance notices and the teacher had sent me a brief email on Wednesday about paying for it so she wouldn't be left out. It didn't really matter—Josie loved going anywhere new. So far, besides a few comments about missing her daddy, this entire visit to Aunt Celia had been an adventure to her.

"Hey Josie, where are we going on our trip today? Do you know?"

"Uhhhhm . . ." She stared absently out the window, and I knew I wasn't getting an answer from her.

"I guess it'll be a surprise, then," I responded, a smile in my voice at her wandering attention.

"I love surprises," she sighed.

"And I love you, baby girl."

When we pulled up at the school, the enthusiastic group of milling children—and far *less* enthusiastic, smaller group of parents clutching coffee cups—waiting next to a couple of school buses told me we were in the right place. Grabbing our sack lunches, I had to hustle to keep up with Josie, who made a beeline for two little girls toward the edge of the group.

"Reesey! Lindsay!" She darted over and the three of them joined in a big group hug, then diffused into giggles about something. It made me smile, and a feeling of relief washed over me. Her desire to wear pigtails this morning also made a lot more sense, once I saw their hair. They were a tiny pigtail gang.

I searched the crowd and spotted her teacher, Ms. Levi, and walked over. "Hi, Ms. Levi. Josie and I are here to check in."

She returned my smile with a cool, calm one. "Awesome, we're just waiting on three more kids and we'll be good to go. Also, you can call me Kath. Have you met the other parent volunteers?"

I followed her gesture to a group of six parents, looking exhausted already, on the outskirts. "Not yet."

"Come on, I'll introduce you. They're mostly great."

"Mostly?" I tried to squash my chuckle at her honesty.

"*Mostly*," she emphasized.

We walked up to a circle of five moms and a dad, and she fired off their names so quickly I only caught Bill, Elaine, and nothing else. I gave them all a stiff wave. "I'm Maggie."

Most responded back with polite nods and waves, but one went straight in for the kill.

"So, new to town? Did your husband get moved here for work?" She arched a perfectly shaped eyebrow at me, then dropped her gaze to my bare left hand.

"No, just me and Josie." I gave her a flat smile, discouraging further questions down that line.

"So, what do you think of town so far?" Bill asked.

"Oh, it's great. I visited a lot as a kid, so it's familiar. Just haven't lived here since I was a baby."

"Celia's your aunt, right? So you're . . . Delia Lee's daughter?"

I tried not to roll my eyes at her use of my mom's middle name. Southerners were weird sometimes. Everyone at home had called my mom Dee. "Yes, that was my mom."

"Oh, I'm so sorry. We all heard about the cancer," Elaine said sincerely, placing a hand on my forearm.

I gave her a polite grimace. "Thanks."

Everyone stood in awkward silence for a moment, but Kath's voice thankfully rang out and broke the tension. "Okay, Ms. Levi's class will be on bus A, right

31

up front. If you're in my class or Mrs. Donahue's, please make a single-file line and we'll get going. Bus B, wait for Mrs. Shreck." She shepherded kids with practiced ease, and they hopped into line like a well-oiled machine.

The parents were slower, but we joined the back of the line. Josie craned her neck before climbing on and waved when she spotted me. I waved back and gave her a thumbs up, and she hopped up the steps with as much spring as a bunny.

It was going to be an interesting day.

The hour and a half drive to the field trip was so loud I didn't have to worry about small talk with the other parents. It was both a relief and headache-inducing. When we passed a green sign painted with "Savannah Wildlife Refuge," my heart leapt into my throat. I turned to Elaine, scrolling on her phone next to me.

"The field trip is at the Wildlife Refuge?"

"Hmm? Oh, yeah. The kids love it. They take the kindergarten class every year, and they love to see the animal rehab center, do the hiking trails, and there's one park ranger who's really great. The kids all love him." She leaned in closer, and dropped her voice to a whisper. "The moms love him too, because that is one fiiiiiiine man. Single, too." She gave me a pointed look, and I must have looked horrified because she laughed and went back to scrolling.

Surely it wasn't Jensen? I mean, what were the odds? No, there could be more than one attractive park ranger. He'd said the park was enormous, and he was working on a new conservation project, not squiring around school kids and—apparently lustful—moms. The bus parked, and I made myself focus on the rowdy children, not the rowdy butterflies rioting in my stomach at the thought of running into Jensen.

Once we'd been split into groups—Elaine and I had five kids to keep an eye on—we went into the welcome center and watched an informational video on the park, its mission, and some of the good conservation work they'd done over the years. It was a neat video, but my eyes kept drifting to the men and women in park ranger uniforms buzzing around the center, hoping to catch sight of Jensen. It was no surprise he wasn't there, and by the time the video ended and the kids were squirming in their seats, I'd reassured myself that he wouldn't be there today.

"Okay, everyone, our dedicated ranger is here to show us around. Please gather your groups and follow us!" Ms. Levi called from the back of the room, and when I finished my head count and turned around, I was shocked to find a beaming Jensen and his popping biceps standing next to Ms. Levi.

"Hey, kids!" He leaned down, closer to their level, sucking them in with his energy. "Who's ready to see some WILDLIFE?!" he hollered.

Every kid in the room screamed in response, and he straightened and pumped a fist in excitement. "All right! That's what I like to hear! I think by the end of the day, you'll all be junior rangers!" He scanned the group while he spoke, and when his eyes landed on me there was a near-imperceptible lift of surprise to his eyebrows. He shot me a quick wink, then continued without missing a beat. "Follow me, kids, I have so much to show you!"

More hoots and hollers ensued as the kids streamed out the doors behind him. I gulped air, steeling myself for his reaction when he put two and two together, and realized that my "it's complicated" meant one of these kids was mine. He'd probably run for the hills. I let it out in a despairing gust, just as Elaine elbowed me in the ribs.

"What did I tell you? The man is a work of art." She kissed her fingers dramatically, then lowered her voice to a whisper, "I saw that wink. Don't get too excited, though. This is my third field trip with the kids, and he's never given any of the moms more than a passing glance." She shook her head.

"Aren't you married?" I asked, pointing to her wedding ring.

"Oh, yeah. But you're not. I can live vicariously through you." She linked arms with me and pulled me along behind our group and into the soft Georgia sunshine. "You could be the one to catch his eye, you never know."

Keeping my mind on the kids was becoming a form of self-torture. We'd followed Jensen—and that far too enticing park ranger uniform—through multiple exhibits, hands-on nature art, and blessedly, *finally* were breaking for lunch at the outdoor picnic area. Elaine and I had settled our group in at a table, and I'd been tasked with refilling all of the water bottles. A good, safe task. Monotonous, even, by the time I'd walked five minutes and around three bends to the nearest fountain. I was on the last water bottle when a throat clearing to my right made me jump.

"Oh, hi, Jensen," I stuttered. "I didn't see you there." I offered him a smile.

"Sorry! I didn't want to startle you and make you spill." He gestured amiably to the water bottle in my hands just as it started to overflow and run down the sides and onto my tennis shoe and the ground.

"Ahh!" I snatched it away and stopped pressing the lever, embarrassment coloring my cheeks. "Thanks."

"You're welcome. Let me get you a paper towel." He jogged to the restrooms across the way, disappeared inside, and a moment later came back with a wad of paper towels. He handed me half. "May I?" he gestured to the bottle, and I handed it to him, so I could dry my soaking shoe.

"So, are you always on field trip duty?" I asked, watching as he grabbed the wet bottle, efficiently wiped down the sides, then screwed the lid back on. He didn't hand it back.

"Not always, but usually. I really love kids, and some of the other rangers really *don't*." He gave me a lopsided grin, and my heart tried to turn into a puddle in my chest. He cared about nature, literally worked to save the environment, was good-looking enough to be a menswear model, *and* he loved kids?

"That's . . . really great." I struggled to think of anything intelligent to say. My brain was doing too many fixated laps about how *way too perfect* he was for me, the Hot Mess Express that I was.

"It is. It's even better than usual, today." He stepped forward, closing the distance between us and pressing the bottle into my hands. Heat licked up my arm as his fingers brushed mine. It shouldn't have made me want to lean into him, but it did.

"Oh, really? Why is that?" The words came out quieter than I intended, and he leaned down to hear them better.

"Hmm? Well, normally I don't get to see you," he whispered back, right next to my ear. The soft rush of his breath on my skin had my heart trying to jackhammer out of my chest, and I didn't dare move, in case he stopped whatever it was he was doing.

I nearly forgot to breathe when he brushed a curl back from my cheek.

"True. That is true," I said on an exhale, still frozen in silent hope. Of what, I didn't let myself linger on.

He pressed a kiss to my cheek. The gentle touch of his soft, warm lips had the butterfly brigade doing loop-de-loops. He pulled back and took in my expression. "You okay there, tiger?" he joked, and I sucked in a lungful of air, swaying towards him like a magnet.

"You just kissed me," I blurted, brain trying to catch up to my ecstatic hormones.

"Just a friendly peck," he agreed.

"It was, uhm, wow," I spluttered, trying desperately to form a coherent thought.

He grinned so wide, it might have split his handsome face in two, and wouldn't that have been a shame? "I agree, it was wow. I'd like to do it again sometime." He reached up and ran a calloused thumb along my lower lip, and suddenly everything clicked into place.

My hand flew to my cheek, and I was torn between panic and exuberance. "I . . . I can't kiss you right now. I'm on my daughter's field trip. Oh my *word*! What if one of the kids saw that? I have to go!" I turned and practically ran away from him, only slowing when I reached the kids' tables.

The five small faces turned to peer at me expectantly, and it took a second to click. *Water bottles. I left the water bottles. Good grief!* I sat the one still clutched in my hands down, and pasted on a smile. "I'll be right back with the rest. Couldn't carry them all!"

"That's why she enlisted me!" A far-too-chipper masculine voice said over my shoulder, and I willed away the raging blush I felt creeping up my neck.

"Ranger Jensen! Ranger Jensen!" The kids all started bouncing in their seats as he held out water bottles for them to grab.

"Will you have lunch with us?" Mason asked.

Jensen ruffled his floppy black hair. "Maybe next time, buddy. It's not my lunch time yet. I have to get back on the road to the pond conservation site we're working on."

"Awww," they all groaned.

I dared a glance at Elaine, and her expression was curious, borderline gloating, as her eyes drilled into me before flitting back to Jensen.

He waved once more to the kids and winked at me again, before striding away through the park. I slumped down onto the bench seat next to Elaine, and she leaned her arm into mine, whispering right into my ear.

"You owe me the rest of that story later. He was giving you a look like he helped you with more than your water bottles. I. Need. Details." She made a chopping motion into her palm.

I snorted but didn't say a word. What could I say, when I was guilty as charged?

Four

The Check Out

When Saturday morning rolled around, I was up bright and early for the breakfast shift. I snuck a kiss onto a sleeping Josie's forehead on the way out the door and said yet another prayer of thanks for my Aunt Celia. She was watching Josie for the day, her helper, Bea, manning the bakery solo so that she could have the whole day to take her to the park, then stop by the restaurant for breakfast to see me before my shift ended. Basically, she was filling the shoes for my mother without a whisper of complaint. Josie had only one living grandmother, but she was even less involved in her life than Carl wanted to be, which was not at all.

I scowled as I drove down the two-lane road, remembering our parting conversation . . .

"I want you out by the end of the week," Carl said, his tone bored as he scrolled through his work phone.

"As in Saturday? That's three days away—where are we supposed to go?" I clutched the handle of my coffee mug so hard, it bit into the palm of my hand, and I worried I'd crush it.

He shrugged, and his blasé attitude about kicking me and our daughter out had me fuming. "I know it's short notice, but frankly if you make it quick for me now, I'll make it quick for you when it's time to file the paperwork. No contest. Josie and you can start fresh . . . wherever you want to be." He waved a hand and then looked straight back down at his phone, dismissing me.

The *only* good thing about the whole mess was that he hadn't tried to fight me for custody of Josie. She was an angel, and frankly, he didn't deserve her. I'd packed as much as I could fit into my car and driven straight to Aunt Celia's house. It was a crash landing, but she made it as easy on us as she could. I would have been up the creek without her. With Mom gone and Dad grieving, I couldn't add to his troubles by showing up there. Aunt Celia had saved our bacon, and I'd never forget her kindness.

41

I blew out a shaky breath as I parked in the lot at Jude's. Even just thinking about Carl and how easily he'd written us off made me angry; a bundle of upset energy that made my hands shake and my blood pressure spike. Dropping my forehead to the steering wheel, I took a few deep breaths through my nose, and slowly blew them out of my mouth. I had to get my head on straight before I could deal with customers. I needed good tips to show income to qualify for a rental, and there was no way I'd be able to do that if I had on my angry face all morning.

Once the anger passed, I hopped out and walked in, ready to get down to business—the business of building a stable life for my daughter and me.

The Saturday morning breakfast rush was intense. Thankfully the fast pace of the restaurant drug me out of my unpleasant thoughts and into the moment, and I buried myself in the work. Aunt Celia and Josie popped in for breakfast, and I took a minute to sit with her while she devoured her rainbow sprinkle pancakes.

"Mom, we're going to the park, and then we're going to the bake shop. Aunt Celia's going to let me design my own cookie flavor." She leaned forward conspiratorially and whispered, "I'm going to pick sprinkle," before shoving a huge bite of pancake into her mouth.

I tugged gently on one of the curls in her ponytail. "I can't wait to try them. But is 'sprinkle' a flavor?" I glanced at Celia, who was sipping her sweet tea with an amused expression.

"It is the way we do it. Isn't that right, Jo-jo?"

"That's right! They're going to be delicious, Mom."

"I have no doubts." *Thank you*, I mouthed to Celia, who waved me off with a smile. Her wistful expression as Josie chattered told me she didn't mind a bit.

After that, it was back into the deep end of the breakfast rush for the next hour. When things finally started to slow, I was dead on my feet, and halfway through my second cup of coffee. I'd found the single chair tucked behind the prep bar—where Sue sometimes sat to prep salads when it had been a long day—and flopped down in it for a moment to catch my breath.

Eyes closed, I was savoring the moment of peace and my last sip of coffee when Janie called for me. I stood, trying to wipe the weariness from my expression, and spotted her next to one of my tables where she was speaking with a new customer. She waved me over and headed back to the front of the restaurant. Dropping my mug into a bus tray, I jogged over to take the newcomer's order, and stopped dead in my tracks.

"Jensen," I blurted, trying to keep the panic out of my voice. What would he think after our last interaction? Would things be weird between us?

"Magnolia," he drawled, my name sounding like honey coming from his beautiful lips.

"I . . . I didn't expect to see you so soon." I tucked a wayward curl behind my ear and resisted the urge to bite my lip. *Why was I so awkward?* I was a grown woman, nearly a divorcée, for Pete's sake! I should be capable of talking to a man—albeit an inconveniently handsome one—without sounding like an idiot.

"No? I thought you might have been expecting me."

"Ah, well, that's true. You do come in a lot. I don't know why I'm so . . . never mind. What can I get you today?"

He chuckled at my ramble. "I'll have coffee, black, with the number three special; hash browns, extra crispy, and over medium eggs."

I scribbled it down and peeked over his shoulder at the menu to see if there were any other options

I was supposed to ask him for the number three. "What kind of toast?"

"Biscuit, please and thank you."

God, did the man say anything without a devious twinkle in his eye? Dangerous. He was dangerous to my heart. "You're welcome, I'll be right back with that."

I did my best to focus on my job, on professionalism, on the state of the flipping union—*anything* but how his lips had felt on my cheek the day before. But it was impossible. I shoved the ticket into the rack with more force than necessary, and Denise gave me a startled look behind the window.

"Sorry," I grumbled and made a beeline for the coffee station. My hands were steady as I poured his cup, despite the fact that I peeked over my shoulder to check on him while I did it. He sat there, a pleasant look on his face, scanning the restaurant and looking out the window. From this angle I could see the sharp angle of his jaw, a bit of light-brown stubble dusting it in a way that made my fingers itch to run across it. I set the pot back on the burner, and carefully walked his cup across the floor to his booth.

"Thanks, Magnolia." He smiled, and took a small sip from the cup. "Do you like coffee?"

I snorted. "I have a six-year-old. Coffee is a food group."

He laughed. "Understood. Would you like to share a cup with me?" He gestured to the other side of his booth.

I nibbled the corner of my lip, and then shook my head no.

He frowned. "Don't want to, or is it more of those *complications* you mentioned?" When I hesitated, he added, "If you really don't want to, I will leave you alone. I'm not one to chase a woman who's uninterested."

I could feel myself wavering. His eyes were sincere; if I told him to shove off, he wouldn't ask again. My heart revolted at the idea. "It's the complications. I really shouldn't."

"But you want to?"

I nodded.

"Well, all right then. Maybe another time." His smile was easy, unoffended that I'd turned him down, and relief flooded my veins.

As I went to wait for his breakfast by the pick-up window, I couldn't help but wonder why I cared so much how Jensen thought of me, and why I'd been disturbed by the idea of him leaving me alone. After delivering his plate, I made myself go behind the prep bar and fill saltshakers, anything to keep my hands busy and not hovering like a lost puppy next to his table while he ate.

Janie walked by and stopped next to me. "I want to train you to use the register, so when your table's ready to cash out, bring him over and I'll teach you."

"Okay, sounds good," I agreed.

Jensen didn't take long, and soon I was bringing his check over and clearing the empty plates. He already had his card ready.

"Ready for me to check you out? Come on over to the register."

He stood and followed me and waited while I walked around behind the cash register. When I looked up at him and reached to take his ticket, he was standing a step or two back hands on his hips.

"Uhm, I need your check back . . ." I looked pointedly to my waiting hand.

He grinned. "I know, I was just letting you finish checking me out first."

"What?" I asked, confused.

He strode forward and pressed the ticket into my palm, the warmth of his fingers sending a zing of excitement up my arm. He leaned in close enough that our foreheads nearly touched, and stage-whispered, "You said you wanted to check me out, so I was letting you get your fill." Then he winked, giving me a playful grin.

"Oh. My. Word." I groaned at the cheesiness, and smacked him lightly on the arm. "Get out of here!" I rolled my eyes just as Janie walked back over.

"What are you two getting up to over here? Is he giving you a hard time? I can throw him out." Her eyes twinkled with merry mischievousness, and I swore I saw the same matchmaking look that Aunt Celia wore on the regular as she elbowed him playfully in the ribs.

"Janie, you wound me. She was flirting with me first, I swear it." He raised his hands, looking the picture of the innocent schoolboy.

"Uh-huh. A likely story. Our Maggie is delightful, and you're not sure what to do about a lady who doesn't chase you first." She tsked playfully and he grabbed his heart as if she'd shot him.

"The service I get, and me a regular customer!"

She just chuckled at his dramatics while showing me how to scan the barcode and enter the payment type. It was easy-peasy, and in a moment we were done. She wandered off to greet a friend across the restaurant.

"See you next time, Magnolia," he said as he pushed his way out the door, our eyes lingering for a long moment before he turned and walked away. The sound of my name in his delicious drawl made me feel things I didn't think I was capable of anymore. And that was the scariest part.

A few days later, I was back at the restaurant for my last shift of the week. Janie grinned at me when she buzzed past to grab a pitcher of tea to help with refills. "You've got a not-so-secret admirer, Maggie. Jensen's here, and requested your section again. Third time this week, isn't it?" She drummed her fingers on the counter and gave me an encouraging smile before heading back to circulate with the pitcher.

I scanned the room and spotted him in his new favorite booth, the one where I'd sat and shared a club sandwich with him. She was right, he'd come in every day this week except Sunday, and every time he requested me. It was flattering, but I was also getting frustrated with myself. I needed to tell him why I hadn't said yes, make him understand why I couldn't get involved with anyone right now. Determined, I crossed the floor with purpose. I was going to explain it to him today, so he didn't waste so much time pursuing me, when I wasn't available.

"Magnolia, how are you today?" His greeting sent a frisson of warmth down my spine, but I ignored it.

"Jensen, fancy seeing you here again. You know, people are starting to talk." Even Aunt Celia, who Janie had filled in on his frequent visits.

"Why, what is there to talk about? Can't a man enjoy Granny's famous sweet tea? Plus, the company here is exceptional." He took a long swig from his glass to punctuate his point, but I drew on my stern mom voice.

"Jensen, I meant it when I said things were complicated, and you coming in here every day is giving people the wrong idea. This won't work."

His eyebrows pulled together in a skeptical frown. "Yes, you keep saying it's complicated, but you haven't said why. Also, I think me coming in here every day is giving people exactly the *right* idea. That I'm interested, and trying to get you to go on a date with me." He leaned forward intently. "You can say yes any time."

I groaned. "It's not—"

"That simple, I know, I know." He sighed, then perked up. "I've got just the thing. Come to dinner with me, and you can explain. All the gory details, no disruptions, and let's see if we can't make it less complicated together."

My jaw dropped. "Isn't that just a date, when I've just said we can't date?"

"No, it's the opposite. It's an un-date. Just dinner between friends, discussing life's complexities."

What was I supposed to say to that? "I think you'll just be disappointed."

He shook his head. "I could never be disappointed in an evening spent with you. Please? Not a date. Just friends. Let me help you uncomplicate your life. It sounds like you could use a hand."

He was so dang sincere. I mean, he was goofy and over the top and ridiculous with his *check me out* jokes sometimes, yes. But his eyes, his face, the intent way he just offered to help me, made it seem like he really wanted to solve it all, make the complexities of my single-parenting and soon-to-be-divorced life vanish into thin air.

"She's thinking about it, folks . . . and the judges say?" His expression lifted hopefully.

"Yes, we can grab a bite to eat. But it's *not* a date. No romance, no candles. Just friends." I gave him my sternest look, so he knew I meant business.

"Yes ma'am. No romance whatsoever . . . unless you say otherwise."

Somehow, that grin on his face told me he wasn't deterred in the slightest by my mom voice. I was in trouble.

FIVE

Not a Date

T hursday morning rolled around, and with it, my first morning sleeping in since we'd come back to Adele. Aunt Celia had taken Josie to school for me, and I had big plans for the day: laundry, and then a trip to the bakery to sample donuts and see if I could lend a hand to repay her for all of her help the last couple of weeks.

I tossed a load in the wash, spruced up my curls, and threw on my favorite blue jeans before heading out for breakfast at the bakery. I was humming along to the radio halfway there when I realized with startling clarity that I was happy this morning. Happier than I'd been in . . . a long time. Longer than I could remember, maybe since Josie was a baby.

Those days had a special sort of magic wrapped around them, and even Carl's presence couldn't sour the memories.

It was a short jaunt to the Sweet Nothings Bake Shop, and the comforting scents of warm baked goods washed over me as the front door bell tinkled at my entrance. I was perusing the glass display case when Bea, Aunt Celia's only employee, pushed her way through the swinging doors from the kitchen.

"Hey, Maggie! How are you today?" Her smile was warm as she wiped floury hands off on a towel hung from her apron.

"I'm good, actually." I smiled back.

"Good, I was hoping you'd settle in and like it here. Actually, Daphne and I were talking about it yesterday. Would you like to join us for our next girls' night? We usually go for hibachi over at the Sushi House, and we'd love to have you."

"Wow, sure. I'd love to, thanks."

"Awesome, we're going Tuesday night. Oh, and we always dress fancy, because it's fun."

I chuckled. I'd have to raid Aunt Celia's closet if they wanted *fancy*. When I left Carl, I gave away all the glitzy clothes he preferred for me, and went back to my roots. "It's a date."

"What can I get you?"

"Hmm, the biggest coffee you've got, and one of those pastries, please." I pointed out a twisty thing dotted with sugared cherries. I had no idea what it was, but if Aunt Celia'd made it, it was guaranteed to be divine.

"Ooh, cherry-almond croissant. Excellent choice." She efficiently plated it, poured me a steaming cup of coffee, and set them both on top of the case for me.

"How much do I owe you?" I pulled out my wallet, and she waved me off.

"On the house; boss's orders."

"She's stubborn." I tucked a ten into the tip jar and was about to grab my pastry when my phone rang. I picked it up and tucked it between my ear and shoulder, so I still had both hands. "Hello?"

"Magnolia, how are you this morning?" Jensen's rich masculine voice rolled over me, rooting me to the spot.

"Jensen, hi. I'm great . . . Uhm, how'd you get my phone number?" I asked belatedly.

"Ahh, I realized that I forgot to ask you before I left the restaurant, so I called Celia. I hope that's okay? She didn't seem to mind."

I bet she didn't, the meddler. "Yes, of course it's fine. I was just surprised."

"Well, I just wanted to call and see what you were doing Saturday for lunch?"

"Ahh, I'm working the breakfast shift Saturday, so I won't be off until two."

"Hmm, I'd say we could have dinner, but you said *no romance* so . . . late lunch? I can pick you up from the restaurant, if you'd like."

I grimaced, imagining myself smelling like food from working all morning. But, it wasn't a date, right? "Sure, that would be great. Though, I can meet you somewhere."

"I don't mind picking you up. See you at two!"

"Okay, bye."

"Bye." I hung up, and set my coffee down to slip the phone into my back pocket.

Bea was still in front of me, wide-eyed and toying with her hand towel. "Was that Jensen Reed?"

I nodded.

"Oh my word, he is such a catch. Is he taking you on a date? That's amazing!" She bounced on the balls of her feet until I shook my head. "Oh, well, what are you doing then?"

"It's just a friend's lunch. I can't date anyone right now, Bea. My divorce hasn't been finalized yet, and I can't get Carl to sign the papers. Plus, I have Josie to focus on, and my life is just complicated right now.

He's a single, good-looking guy. He doesn't want all this drama." I waved my hand vaguely.

She shrugged. "Everyone's got something, though. Just because he doesn't have an ex-wife and a kid doesn't mean his life is perfect." A timer began to beep in the kitchen, and she glanced that way.

"Well, that's true. But still. I'm a lot right now. Anyways, it's just lunch. As friends."

She tossed the towel over her shoulder. "Just don't sell yourself short. You've been through a lot, but that doesn't diminish your awesomeness. It makes you extra awesome. Let him decide what he does and doesn't want." She waggled her fingers at me to say goodbye, and pushed back into the kitchen to deal with whatever was beeping.

Friday saw me browsing another page of real estate listings and marking down more for the realtor. There was also a call from the mediator, stating that Carl still hadn't signed, and had some issues with the agreement. She'd ended with, "You should be expecting his call," which was a sure-fire way to spoil the rest of the day.

By the time Saturday rolled around, frustration with Carl—who *still* hadn't bothered to call—and nerves about my "friend lunch" with Jensen were battling for supremacy. I picked at my breakfast and struggled to remember drink orders half the morning. By the time my shift ended, I was relieved to be done for the day, and nerves about my lunch with Jensen were front and center. I hung my apron up at the restaurant, ran into the bathroom to check my hair—and that the mascara I'd applied before my shift hadn't smudged—before walking out the front door.

There he was, big white truck idling already. I checked the clock. One fifty-nine, which meant he'd come early. I walked around to the side, but before I could reach the handle to open it myself, he'd hopped down from the driver's seat, and jogged around to open it for me.

"You look beautiful today, Magnolia." He greeted me with a soft smile.

"Thank you, Jensen. You look nice, too." And he really did. He'd traded that distracting park ranger's uniform for khaki shorts and a deep green polo which brought out the color of his eyes, clearly putting effort into this *not*-date. His hair was damp and freshly combed, and I was tempted to lean over and muss it, just a little. I fought the urge down as I climbed into his truck and he carefully shut the door for me, and then climbed back in on his side. In our ten-year marriage, I don't think Carl had ever once opened the car door for me.

The radio played soft country tunes as we pulled out, and I realized that I had no idea where we were going. "So, what's the plan for lunch?" I asked, using my best casual tone. I wiped my sweaty palms on my jeans, and knew it wasn't likely I'd actually *feel* relaxed any time soon. Just sitting next to the man had me wound tight.

"I was wondering when you'd ask. Have you heard of the Double F Ranch? It's a little ways outside of town."

"No . . . do they have a restaurant there?" I asked, confused.

He chuckled. "Not quite. But my friends, the Ferguson brothers, own it."

"Makes sense, given the name," I joked.

"Funny and beautiful. The total package." He reached over and squeezed my hand appreciatively, but didn't give me time to object to his compliment before continuing. "I wanted to take you somewhere nice that you wouldn't feel like you're under the town microscope, and where we'd be able to talk without interruptions."

My heart melted another degree at his thought-fulness. He'd really been listening to me, and he'd picked up on my discomfort more than I'd realized. "A tall order," I murmured.

"I'm up for the challenge. I called my buddy Scott, and he said absolutely we could use their place. So, we're having a picnic. I hope you like fried chicken."

"I love fried chicken. Did you order it from the diner?"

"Uh, not quite."

Was that *embarrassment* I detected in his tone? My interest was piqued, now. "So, where did you get it?"

"My mom helped me make it."

A chuckle escaped me before I reined it in. "You just dialed her up and she made you fried chicken?"

"Not quite. I had to promise some bonus yard work for her next weekend. She's a smart business-woman. I'm going to be trimming her crepe myrtles for four hours."

"It sounds like it would have been easier to buy the chicken."

"Maybe, but you're worth the effort, Magnolia." His tone was dead serious, and butterflies took wing in my stomach once again. "Besides, nobody else makes it like Mama."

"So, what does your mom think you need fried chicken for, exactly?"

"Impressing you. I tried to tell her that we're just friends, but she didn't buy it." He shrugged, not seeming the least bit ashamed of himself.

I shook my head at his willingness to talk to his family about me, when I had done nothing but push him away so far. I certainly hadn't run home to Aunt Celia and gushed my feelings to her, though this un-date would be worth gushing over, and it hadn't even started. I just hoped he didn't leave disappointed today.

The drive out of town was lovely, and while he said it was a ways, the time flew by as we chatted and, to my surprise, my nerves slowly faded away. He was playful and goofy at times, but there was also something about him that drew me in, and made me feel comfortable. As we bumped down the driveway and under the Double F Ranch sign, I was eagerly looking forward to our picnic.

"Wow, that is a gorgeous home." I spotted a sprawling ranch house off to the right, surrounded by flat, cross-fenced fields with red cows roaming here and there.

"Yeah, that's Brent's design. He's a custom builder, and he's built some really beautiful homes all over the county."

"I thought you said your friend's name was Scott?"

"They're brothers. Scott's my age, Brent's younger. There are actually five Ferguson brothers."

We drove past the beautiful home, and past a thatch of woods. In the distance, I spotted another clearing with a pretty white gazebo. "Do they all live out here? There's certainly plenty of space."

"Four of them do."

"That must be nice, to have so much family close."

"Yeah, they are very lucky."

"What about you? Big family? Small family?" I asked, realizing I actually knew very little about him, except his job and his love of Jude's cooking—and, now, that his mom had skills frying up chicken.

"Small. Just me, my parents, and my sister."

"You're lucky. I always wanted a sister."

"So, no siblings?"

"Nope, just me. And now Josie, my daughter."

"What about your parents? Do they live close?"

"My dad lives up in Virginia, and we lost my mom to cancer two years ago. He took it hard, and he's more or less buried himself in work ever since." I thought of their home, always so vibrant when Mom was in it, but it felt painfully empty now.

"I'm sorry to hear that. I can't imagine how hard it must have been to lose her, and with your daughter so young at the time."

"It was hard, but taking care of Josie pulled me through."

We grew quiet as he pulled up to the gazebo, and parked the truck. "Are you hungry, or do you want to explore first?"

"I'm starved."

"Well then, let's get this picnic started!" He climbed down from the truck, and walked around to hold my door for me on the way out, too. He offered his hand, and comforting warmth enveloped my palm as I stepped out of the truck. I felt a pang of sadness when he released me, but pushed that down. I might not have been ready to date, but that didn't mean I couldn't enjoy time spent with a friend. Even single mothers were allowed to have those.

He pulled a large backpack and a small cooler from the back seat before leading me into the tiny gazebo. It was white, with blooming morning glories crawling up each of the posts, and some dangling overhead. Sweet perfume filled the air from the blooms, and I inhaled the heady scents happily. A picnic table had been set in the middle of the gazebo, complete with a blue mason jar stuffed with wildflowers and cloth napkins stuffed into antique silver rings.

Jensen got right to work setting out tupperwares of food, and delicious scents competed with the flowers as he opened each one and set them out.

After the fried chicken, watermelon slices, potato salad, and cornbread muffins, I lost track of what else he pulled from the bag. I was so overwhelmed by his thoughtfulness, and the amount of effort he'd gone to just to sit down and have lunch with me.

"Wow, you've outdone yourself, Jensen, really. You did not have to go to this much trouble. I'd have been happy with a sandwich."

He shook his head in amusement. "I believe you. But I wanted to do this for you. Make it special. Is that okay?"

"Yes, of course. It all looks wonderful."

"Good, I hope you like it." He passed me a plate, and waited for me to serve myself before he added anything to his own plate.

Once we'd both settled in and had taken a few bites, he asked the question I'd been dreading for two days.

"So, tell me about your complications. Don't leave anything out, I don't scare easily."

I swallowed a bite of corn bread and washed it down with my lemonade, buying myself a little time to think. Where did I even begin? "Well, you saw me at the field trip, so you know I have a daughter. Josie. She's six."

"And adorable, yes."

"She is, isn't she?" I drew in a shaky breath, bolstered by thoughts of my girl. "Well, her father is the main complication. He's . . ." I stopped, unsure how much detail to give him. Going on about my ex seemed like a bad idea.

"Still in the picture?" Jensen prompted.

"No, he's not. We're getting divorced, and he's been completely hands-off since he asked us to leave."

Jensen set his fork down, and leaned forward on his elbows, plate abandoned. "He asked you to leave? Your home?"

"Yes, after he filed for divorce, it was like he flipped a switch. One day, the devoted father and husband, the next . . . not." I shrugged, struggling to describe Carl. He'd never been super dad, but he'd been around. Mildly interested, never rude or abusive, more absent and inattentive.

"How long were you two together?" His tone was carefully neutral, and I couldn't read much on his face.

"Ten years."

He ran a hand over his face, as if he was weary just listening to the story. "Why'd he do it? Do you know?"

Embarrassment flooded me at imagining telling this gorgeous man about my husband's infidelity,

64

and I looked down at the dainty cloth napkin in my lap. A soft touch on my chin startled me into looking up, into his piercing green eyes.

"Hey, it's okay. You don't have to tell me if you don't want to. But you can, and I won't judge."

I squared my shoulders, and told him the rest. About the new woman, about him asking us to leave, and about having to uproot Josie. Our crash landing at Celia's, and my new job at the restaurant while we looked for a little place we could afford on our own. When I was done, I took a pointed swig of my lemonade, and braced myself for his reaction.

"Well, he's a bastard for leaving you two. And a blind idiot, because whoever he found couldn't be better than you."

Shocked, my eyes flew up from the rim of my glass to his face. He was dead serious.

"And I'll *never* understand a man that abandons his children." Anger crossed his face for the first time, but he tucked it back away. "Sounds like you're better off without him, if that's who he is. But I'm sorry you've had to go through it." He squeezed my hand supportively, and tears flooded my eyes in gratitude.

He hadn't judged me. He hadn't looked at me as if I were less than, because I couldn't keep my husband happy. He hadn't run screaming at the news that I was a newly-single mother. I tried to keep the tears from falling, but to my utter mortification one slid free. Then another.

"Hey, hey now. Come here." He came around the picnic table, sat next to me on the bench, and pulled me into a hug. I buried my face into his shoulder, and the rest of the tears came unbidden.

"I'm going to soak your shirt," I hiccupped, the words muffled against his shoulder.

"Shh, don't worry about that." He rubbed my back in slow circles, and slowly the tears subsided. I focused in on the routine motion, the soothing cadence bringing my breathing back to normal. My focus gradually shifted away from the painful emotions, and to the heat radiating from his muscular arm, combined with the nice scent of him. He smelled like pine trees and pure masculinity, and I wanted a candle made out of his scent so I could be surrounded by it all the time.

When I pulled back, he cupped my face in his hands, running his thumbs under my eyes to wipe away the last of the tears. I rubbed gently at the wet spot on his shirt, and he shook his head at me, an amused glint at my feeble attempt to wipe away the evidence.

"Sorry, I'm not really all that sad about Carl, but sometimes the emotions catch me by surprise. I'm angry, more than anything. This wasn't the life I wanted for Josie, or for myself."

"No apologies. You're allowed to feel however you want. Personally, I'd like to punch the man."

I chuckled. "Sometimes I feel the same way. Aunt Celia would be appalled."

"Mm, I'm not. I'm glad you're feisty." His look grew heated, and his thumb traced down to the corner of my lips, drawing lazy lines across my cheek, and back down to tease my bottom lip. Warmth flared everywhere he touched, and a sigh escaped my lips.

I leaned into the touch, wanting more of him. More of his fingers, more of his warmth, more of his intoxicating scent. He closed the distance between us and pressed a kiss to my forehead. The touch was gentle, but I felt like I'd been branded—changed by him. He pulled away and held my gaze.

"Can I kiss you?"

"You've kissed me twice now."

"True, but I want to feel your lips on mine more than I want my next breath. It seemed like I should ask permission, since this *isn't* a date."

My lips parted in surprise at his brazenness, but I felt myself nodding, wanting his, too.

He didn't waste another second, swooping in to claim me in an enveloping kiss. I lost track of time, knowing nothing at all except him. His warmth.

His strength. His soft lips molding to mine. When he pulled away and we locked eyes again, I knew. My mind, my heart, my very being were already wrapped up in this man, and we weren't even dating. I was in so much trouble.

SIX

Lawyer Friend

After our lunch—and whatnot—the drive back to
town was surreal. We were in a happy bubble,
not at all what I expected given what I'd told him.
Somehow, he'd taken in all my baggage, all my shortcomings, and hadn't been scared off. He was even
more miraculous than I'd thought.

We were just pulling into the restaurant parking
lot so I could get my car and head home, when my
phone rang. Carl's name flashed on the screen, and
I groaned.

"What's wrong?"

"It's him. Carl. I've been waiting on a call for two
days to discuss the divorce papers he still hasn't
signed, but it's awful timing. I'll call him back." I was

about to click the reject button when he interrupted.

"Don't, it's okay. You can answer."

"Are you sure? I don't want to drag you even further into the mess that is my life."

He locked eyes with me as he put the truck in park. "I'm sure."

I swiped the green icon, accepting the call. "Carl."

"Maggie. What are you trying to pull?"

"What do you mean?" Unease washed through me at the accusation in his tone. I wasn't trying to pull anything, except finalizing the divorce he'd sprung on me.

"The divorce settlement? Outrageous child support. *Alimony*?"

"Carl, I don't know what the problem is. The mediator looked at our assets and made recommendations. I changed nothing."

He scoffed, and my blood pressure started to rise in anger. "What makes you think you deserve that much of *my* money? You barely worked our entire marriage. I supported you, I supported Josie. You lived a charmed life, and now you think you deserve more than half? For what? So you can run off and hate-spend my money? I don't think so. You want Josie, you're going to drop it. If I've got to pay for her, she's coming to live with me. If you can't support her anyways, you're not very fit to keep her, now, are you?"

"No! You swore that if we left, you wouldn't fight me for Josie. You gave us *days* to move, so you could move your new lady-friend in. Now you're going to go back on your word, and threaten me for custody? Over money?"

"It's not a threat. It's a promise. You fix this settlement, or you lose Josie. I've got the job, the house, and the means to support her. What have you got? No. You don't deserve half, and I'm not paying a dime in alimony. Fix it."

He hung up the phone, and for the second time in the same day, tears flooded my eyes. This time, they were angry. "Son of a gun!" I resisted the urge to throw the phone, barely.

"Did he just threaten you?" Jensen's voice was eerily calm, and I could feel the storm on the edges of his tone.

"I'm not sure." My hands shook again, and I clenched them into fists to stop it. "Yes. He implied that if I didn't ask for less money in the settlement he'd tell the judge I was unfit and couldn't support Josie. I didn't even draw it up! The mediator said what was fair." I slammed my fist down on the arm rest, needing to vent the anger somewhere.

"He threatened to take custody of your daughter because he's too cheap to pay you what you deserve for putting up with his sorry rear end for ten years?"

"Like all she's worth to him is as a bargaining chip," I said, disgusted.

"Where does he live again? I need to pay him a visit."

"Jensen, no. I will figure something out."

"Just one good punch. It would be therapeutic."

I huffed. "Maybe, but it wouldn't solve anything." I slumped forward, dropping my head into my hands. "What am I going to do, Jensen? How am I going to get a house if I don't get that money? I just started my job. I need money for a down payment, or at least a deposit on a decent rental." My chest grew tight with worry, and now I wanted to sob for another reason. I wasn't getting off Aunt Celia's couch any time soon, but I'd die before I'd let him have Josie.

"He is not going to stiff you, or get Josie," he crooned, rubbing my shoulder.

I took a few deep breaths to steady myself, and did my best to look self-assured, even though I felt a million miles from it. Josie stuck with Carl full-time would be my worst nightmare come to life, and I would never forgive myself if I somehow let that happen. No, I'd do whatever it took.

"No, he's not," I agreed.

"What can I do to help?"

"Nothing for now. I'm going to have to speak with the mediator, and make a game plan. And I've got to find a house, ASAP." Which stunk, because I couldn't afford much on my own right now. Aunt Celia had offered to pitch in so I could afford something nicer, and I might be forced to accept. I needed there to be no doubt whatsoever that Josie was better off with me.

"I know a really awesome realtor; I could give her a call," he offered.

"That's sweet of you, but Aunt Celia's already got me hooked up with someone. Really, it'll be okay. I dealt with him for ten years, I just have to get through one last hurdle." I squared my shoulders, and I meant it. "Thank you for lunch today, it was wonderful. And the kiss . . ." I trailed off, unsure what to say. It had been mind-blowing.

"It was spectacular, just like the company." He reached up and traced the corner of my mouth with his thumb again, drawing a shudder out of me with the tiny motion. I reached for the door handle—not wanting to make a scene kissing him in the parking lot where I worked—but he was out and jogging around to open it for me before I could blink.

"I hope we can do it again sometime soon and make it official when you're ready," he said as he helped me down from the truck.

"Jensen, I don't know if that's going to be a good idea anytime soon. With all this mess with Carl now, things will be even *more* complicated. I don't even know when I'll be officially divorced, and I don't want to string you along, or mire you in the hot mess that is my life right now." I ran a frustrated hand through my curls, probably causing a wave of frizz, but I didn't care.

"Hey, you're not hearing me today. I don't care. I want to support you, and I don't care how messy it is. What you want, you'll get. If you're comfortable with hanging out as friends, that's what we'll do. If you only want to see me when I come into the restaurant and wave across the room, that's what we'll do. If you're ever ready for more . . . you say the word, and I'm there." He grinned, not put off by my reticence in the least, and pulled me into a friendly side hug.

He didn't suffer from lack of confidence, I had to give him that. I sank into his side, bolstered by the warmth and comfort that was Jensen. I snuck one last sniff of his glorious scent, and then forced myself to step back. "Friends. We can be friends. I like you, and despite feeling like it's not worth the effort for you, well, you're grown. If you say you're up for it, I'll believe you."

"I'm up for it. You ever need some kisses to tide you over, superwoman, I'm up for that too." His wink made me blush like a teenager. "See you tomorrow? Lunch shift?" The grin he shot me wasn't dampened by the ugliness of dealing with my ex, and I was grateful that things still felt the same between us.

"Deal," I agreed, shooting him a smile. His flirtatious energy was infectious, even with the dark cloud of Carl looming overhead. He backed out of the space after I got into my car, and as I pulled out of the lot, Janie caught my eye waving from the doorway.

She ran over, so I rolled down my window. "Can you come in for a minute, dear? The checks came in, and if you hurry you might make the bank before it closes."

"Sure, I'll just go find a spot."

"Ahh, leave it here. It's just for a minute."

I left the car right outside the front door and followed her into the already-familiar restaurant. The smells of good old-fashioned southern food were comforting, and I needed all the comfort I could get right now. I tried to shove it out of my mind, but Carl's threats scared me. Josie was my life.

Janie dug through the pile of envelopes until she spotted mine. "Here you go, Maggie. I know it's not much. I hope it's been a good change for you, coming back to Adele." She looked up, and spotted my sober expression. "Honey, what's wrong? Are you not enjoying the job? You won't hurt my feelings if you don't want to stick around. Waitressing isn't for everyone." She leaned forward and rubbed my forearm, and I had to choke back a sob.

"No, it's not that. You've been great. My husband called, and he won't sign the divorce papers. He says If I don't drop all the financial requests, he'll fight me to take Josie. I don't know what to do. I can barely afford a cheap place to live, let alone a lawyer. But I think I need a lawyer, don't I? If mediation isn't going to work." I sniffled, trying desperately not to break down in the middle of Jude's.

Janie's gaze narrowed and turned icy, and she turned over her shoulder to holler, "Beau! Come here!" She turned back to me and ushered me gently to the nearest empty booth. "Hold on one second dear, I'll get you some tea. No, wait, you like coffee. One second."

She vanished, and I dropped my head into my hands again. I was so tired, and the fight had just begun.

She reappeared a moment later, mug and a whole pot of coffee in hand, Beau hot on her heels. She poured me a fresh cup and slid into the booth next to me, gesturing for Beau to sit across from us. I took a grateful sip, and she put on her stern voice. "It's time to call Lawrence. We need a favor."

His eyebrows rose, but he didn't argue. Apparently, that voice meant business. He whipped out his phone, dialed a number, and waited for it to ring.

"Hey Lawrence, Janie and a friend need to speak with you." He punched a button and set it in the middle of the table, on speaker.

"Janie, how are you, beautiful?"

"Just fine, Lawrence. But we need your help. We've got a new employee in the middle of a divorce, and her ex is a real S-O-B. Cheater. Threatening her. Trying to swindle her out of the family finances and trying to take custody of a girl he's never cared for a day in his life. I would consider it a personal favor if you helped her out." She wrapped an arm around my shoulders and gave me a squeeze. I held my breath for an answer, and I didn't know this Lawrence from Adam.

"Well now, you know I can't say no to a favor for my best sister-in-law, now, can I?"

"No, you cannot. When can you be here?"

"I can't drive down until Friday, but I can start today. Have her send me the settlement statement, and I'll take a look and file an updated petition tomorrow morning. What's her name?"

"It's Maggie. Magnolia Abbott," I spoke up.

"Maggie, don't you worry about a thing. I'll be up from Atlanta this weekend, and we'll get this taken care of. Don't speak with him again, and if anyone tries to contact you, have them call my office. There's one thing I don't take lightly, and that's a man who thinks he can push women around. He's going to get what he deserves. I promise."

"Thank you, Mr. Jude."

"Call me Lawrence, honey. We'll talk soon." With that, he hung up and I turned grateful eyes on Janie and Beau.

"Your brother is a lawyer?"

Beau sighed. "Yeah, a real uppity one over in Atlanta. Rich as Solomon and thinks himself every bit as wise." He snorted. "He forgets I shared a room with him, and I remember the time he broke his ribs jumping into the swimming hole and hitting the bank. But, I'll say this, he's good at his job. He'll take real good care of you, don't you worry."

"I probably can't afford him, though. I don't have to tell you that—you know my situation. I work here and live on my aunt's couch." Shame washed over me at my circumstances.

"Honey, don't look ashamed, and don't worry about the money. It'll all work out."

I hoped so, I really did.

SEVEN

House Shopping

T hat night I updated a very concerned Celia on the situation, and she went into hyper drive, determined to have me in a house by the weekend no matter the cost. I hated taking money from her, but she insisted on giving me the first & last month's rent I needed to get into a place immediately. I swore to myself I'd pay her back every cent, once we were on our feet. And I'd made good on that promise. We would get on our feet because I wouldn't stop working until we were.

The next morning the plan went into motion, and I was picking up extra shifts at the restaurant, and meeting with the realtor in the afternoon. She had a mile-long list of houses to show me, and I was ready.

I would be picking something today and figuring out a move by this weekend.

Of course, I had no furniture or anything else to stock this new house, but that was a problem for Saturday. I blew out a breath and walked out of the restaurant with my head held high. No Jensen today, since I'd changed to the early morning shift so I could be off early to find a house. I'd felt silly, but texted him anyway to let him know I wouldn't be there when he came in for lunch. He thanked me, and wished me luck on the house hunt.

It felt a little like I was holding my breath for the other shoe to drop with him. Could he really be so understanding? Could he really accept me, imperfect as I was, when it seemed he had his whole life in order? Only time would tell. Pushing thoughts of Jensen aside, I headed over to the first listing on Green Street. The street was nice, tree-lined and with massive houses lining either side. As I drove past one brick stunner after another, I had a sinking feeling that I could not afford this house. Nonetheless, it was on the list, so I pulled up. The house for rent wasn't as large as some of the others, so it was possible it could be on the stretch end of my budget.

I climbed from the car and took in the jasmine-wrapped picket fence, and I had to admit it was lovely. Josie would love sniffing the flowers, and hunting for fairy rings. We might even be able to get a puppy, if dogs were allowed. She'd always wanted a pet, but Carl wasn't an animal person. I sighed as I walked up the front steps, where the door was already open.

I knocked timidly, and a strong feminine voice called from one of the bedrooms.

"Maggie? Come on in, sugar. Celia told me you had a deadline, so I went ahead and opened it up for you." She walked from the room, and I took in the statuesque woman. She was in her mid-fifties if I had to guess, but her hair was big and blonde, and she had the presence to match it.

"I'm Leeann, the realtor. Don't be shy, now, we've got eight properties to see today. Isn't this one a beauty? It was built in the fifties, and they don't make 'em like this anymore. The wood floors are original, freshly refinished. It's a three bed, two bath, with a bonus room." She gestured to a sun-drenched room that begged me to linger, but guided me past it and into the kitchen. It was gorgeous, too. "The kitchen's been fully remodeled, but they've kept all of that original charm. Dark stainless appliances are a surprisingly good complement to the cottage style. Unusual, but this designer pulled it together and made it work."

She was right, but the stunning fixtures and silky-smooth stone countertops just underlined that this place had to be out of my price range. She quickly led me past two "kids' rooms" as she called them, and to the owner's suite. It took up the entire rear of the house, and overlooked a sprawling, fenced yard. She was telling me something, but I was too caught up in the daydream that was this house to catch most of it.

". . . and the bathroom's been fitted with a soaker tub, separate walk-in shower, and dual sink vanity. Really, this is the most modern, upgraded home on your list. Several of the others are in need of a bit of repair."

"Yes, I know, but I'm on a tight budget. This can't be in my price range, is it?"

"Well . . . not *strictly*, but Celia added it to the list. She indicated that if you liked it, she'd make up the difference. A generous offer."

"How far over?"

"Well," she hemmed and hawed, not wanting to answer, but I just stared her down. "Eight hundred a month."

"Oh, Celia." I couldn't help the sigh. It was too much. "No, I am going to stand on my own two feet. Let's see the next place that *is* in the budget, please."

"All right, honey, give me just a moment to lock up." She zipped off, shutting off the lights as she went. I got back into my car and, after she locked the front door, we headed to the next property on the list.

Two and a half hours later, I was worn out and bordering on despair. We'd seen seven more properties, each one worse than the last. Leaky, moldy. Washboard roads, and skeevy neighbors—they ran the gamut of issues, even though they'd looked fine in the listing photos. Of course, photos can't convey the deep stench of cat pee, now, can they?

We'd seen everything in my price range, but Leeann said she knew of an off-market property that might be a fit, and I sent up a silent prayer as I pulled onto the street that it would be serviceable. I didn't want Aunt Celia to throw even more money at my problems, and I would feel like a failure if I couldn't do this myself. Huckleberry Road wasn't as fancy as Green Street had been, but it was charming. Modest but clean homes lined each side, and they were unique, built over a span of years rather than a single cookie-cutter mold. Bright, cheerily painted doors lined the way, and when I pulled up at 2341 Huckleberry, I caught my breath.

The home was old—there was no mistaking the Victorian design—but well-maintained. The wrap-around porch had a swing that looked like it had a few good creaking years left in it, and the front door was a deep green. As I walked up the steps, it was instant love. Leeann had the door code punched in before I'd finished taking in the porch, and it only got better when I walked inside. The entryway was quaint but lovely. A large, framed mirror hung to one side over a dainty table for dropping keys and purses. The floors were burnished pine, and sunlight poured in from all the windows. The kitchen was small but lovely, with creamy tiles framing the deep sink and dark fixtures accenting the whole thing. Leeann led me through the rooms—it was another three bed, two bath home—each one small but nicely decorated. One even had a pretty white sleigh bed that Josie would love.

"It's staged, right? So they'll be removing the furniture?" I gestured to the pretty bed, done up in a frilly comforter with pink decorative pillows.

"Oh, well, they can if you don't like it, of course, but it's set to be rented furnished. There's a damage deposit, but if you like it, all of the furnishings except the living room set will stay." She smiled, and I knew she could tell I liked the place. Loved it, really.

The third bedroom was smaller than the grand suite at Green street, but the shape was interesting, and from the outside this had been a turret. The idea of having my own princess tower was amusing.

"Okay, so how far over my budget is this place?" I asked, planting my hands on the counter when we made our way back to the kitchen, bracing for the bad news. If I had to go back to one of the seven deadly housing sins I'd seen prior after this place, I'd cry.

"Well, it is a bit above your price range. However, it's privately owned, and the owner is aware of your situation. He is sympathetic, and willing to write a graduated lease with you, so that over a three-year period you can work up to market rent. The entire first year, he's agreed to lower the rent to your stated budget. Assuming you're planning to stay a while, of course?"

My jaw dropped, shocked at my good fortune. Maybe I should have been embarrassed that the landlord was essentially taking pity on me—Lord help us all survive small-town gossip—but I couldn't find it in myself to care. We had had a hard run lately, so I'd take the olive branch he offered, and not look back. "Where do I sign?"

The rest of the week flew by in a blur. Leeann prepared a lease for the mystery landlord, I worked doubles at the restaurant every single day, and by the time my four o'clock appointment to meet her and sign the lease rolled around I was dead on my feet, but proud. I'd earned enough this week to buy myself a second-hand couch and pay the utility deposits to get a new account set up. I'd never had a utility account in my name before, and I was proud of myself. I was a little behind the curve in my thirties, but I was making up ground one day at a time.

When I passed Leeann Celia's check for the first month's rent and deposit, I swallowed hard. It was a lot of money, but Celia had been insistent. My savings account was tiny, with only what I'd saved in my few weeks working at Jude's so far, and she wanted me to save it for a rainy day. *Rainier* day.

As Leeann slid me the keys and walked me through the lease, the payment schedule, the pet guidelines, three-year term, and unexpected bonus option to purchase at the end of the lease term, it was easy to feel like I'd finally hit a sunny patch.

The final page awaited my signature and had already been signed by the owner-slash-landlord.

I skimmed the page and froze on the name. His name. I met Leeann's eyes; the question clear in my gaze.

"Honey, Jensen asked me not to tell you first. He wanted you to give the idea a fair shake, and he knew you wouldn't like the idea of him helping out. Stubbornly sweet, my son."

Jensen owned the dream house? And this was the mother who'd made us not-date fried chicken?

"I need a minute. I need to make a phone call." I gave her a smile, though it was paper thin, and escaped to the front porch to call Jensen.

He picked up on the first ring, and I could hear the smile in his tone when he spoke, "Magnolia, to what do I owe this unexpected pleasure?"

"Your last name is Reed? Your *mother* is the realtor you were going to recommend?"

"Yeah, that's her. It's not surprising Celia sent you to her; she's the only one in town."

"You own this house. Jensen, I can't accept charity from you." I ran my hands through my hair, disrupting my tight curls once again.

"It's not charity, Magnolia. It's a helping hand. There's a difference. You're going to pay rent and have a signed lease, like any tenant. It's one hundred percent on the up and up," he insisted, growing serious.

"I feel funny about it. Leeann . . . your mom said this house was off the market. Why was it off market?"

He sighed. "Because I had planned for it to be a flip house. But, a rental is an equally good investment, with a long-term payoff."

"You remodeled this place?" I turned back towards the house, my eyes going over the lovingly refinished porch, the minute details perfect.

"With the help of my buddy Brent, yeah. He's got the eye for these kinds of projects."

"It's not going to fall down on us, is it?" I asked wryly.

"Magnolia Abbott, I am offended," he said, but he didn't sound offended in the least. "Are you going to sign the lease, or are you going to be stubborn?"

Now it was my turn to sigh. "I'm going to sign the lease, Jensen. I hope we don't regret it."

"We won't. I'm glad you're going to be staying there. It's a nice place for you and little Josie. You deserve it, Magnolia. You deserve all the good things life has to offer, including a place for you and your daughter to call your own."

"Thank you, Jensen." My words came out choked by tears. When did I start crying so much? I vowed to stop while I dashed them away and walked back in. This man was ruining me, but what a way to go.

EIGHT

Legally Broke

M y Saturday morning shift at the restaurant was a necessary torture, when all I wanted to do was get us moved into the Huckleberry house. I couldn't slack off on work now, when I had a house to pay for, a lawyer to meet—that I couldn't afford—and a burning need to prove I could care for Josie without Carl. I wasn't going to give him a leg to stand on in front of a judge if it killed me. I was hanging up my apron at the end of the breakfast rush when Janie walked into the back room.

"Oh, good, you're still here!" she enthused, and I tried to suppress a groan. I appreciated all the extra hours they'd thrown my way, but today was moving day, and that was top priority.

"Yes, but I'm on my way to get moved in!" I made sure to sound extra chipper, so she'd know I was excited to get going.

"How fun! I won't keep you, I just wanted to see if you'd be willing to work a charity event we have coming up? There's no hourly wage, but you'll get to keep all of your tips."

"Uhm, sure? What's the event?"

"Oh, who knows! The town benevolence committee can't decide. All I know is there will be food, and where there is food, we need servers. I'll keep you posted on the details. Now, off you go! Take pictures for us!"

"I will, for sure." I bustled out before anything else could keep me from my task. I climbed into the car, slid it into reverse, and the phone rang. I stifled a groan, but when I saw the Atlanta area code, I forced myself to pick it up.

"Hello?"

"Hello, Maggie?"

"Yes, Mr. Jude?"

"Ahh, call me Lawrence. I'm in town, and wondering if you're ready to discuss your case? I'd like to give you an update, and some next steps."

"Of course, Lawrence. When would you like to meet?"

"I'm available now. Doesn't your aunt own the bake shop in town? Sweet something?"

"Sweet Nothings. Yes, that's Aunt Celia's place."

"Perfect. I'll meet you there in five."

He hung up, and I resisted the urge to bang my forehead on the steering wheel. It was important, and if he thought he could help, that was another huge win for keeping custody of Josie. I blew out a couple of deep breaths, and then headed to the bakery.

When I walked in the front door, I saw that I'd beaten him there. So, I ordered a cup of coffee—caffeine was essential to divorce proceedings—and picked a large table near the windows to wait for him.

I didn't wait long. A silver fox in a flashy blazer walked in a few moments after I sat down, his eyes raking over the bakery as if it were familiar to him. His steely gaze came to rest on me, and he inclined his head in a nod before crossing the polished floors to where I sat.

"Maggie?"

"Yep, that's me." I stood and extended a hand, which he encased in a firm handshake. "Thank you for meeting me, I really appreciate it."

"It's no trouble at all. Mind if I order myself a cup before we get started?" He gestured to the mug.

"Not at all, want me to get it for you?"

He gestured for me to stay seated, and walked across to the register. Aunt Celia backed through the swinging doors, drying her hands on a pink striped towel.

"Just a moment, and I'll be right with you."

"Take your time, I've been waiting since high school."

Aunt Celia froze, and turned carefully to face the man leaning casually across her work counter. "Well, Lawrence Jude, as I live and breathe. What are you doing back in town? I thought you were too high-falutin' to grace Adele with your presence anymore, now that you're a big-city lawyer."

"Ouch, straight for the jugular, Celia. Where are those dainty Southern manners you're known for?"

She snorted, and lifted a single manicured brow. "Really, Lawrence? You must not remember me as well as you thought."

He grinned as she picked up a coffee pot, not even asking his order. She fixed him a cup, and passed it across the counter. "Well, are you going to tell me what's brought you back to town, or do I have to guess? If I recall, you did love for things to be more mysterious than they needed to be." She drummed her nails on the counter as I watched their exchange with rapt attention.

"Why, your niece, of course." He gestured mag-nanimously to where I sat, and I proffered a hesitant wave towards Celia, her face unreadable.

"Good, she could use a skilled lawyer, and she wouldn't let me help her hire one. Take care of my niece, or I'll gut you like a fish. Josie is the closest thing I've got to a granddaughter, and if you let that weasel Carl within a hundred feet of her, all the tall buildings in Atlanta won't be enough to hide you."

He shook his head, not in the least put off by her gruff threats. "Yes ma'am." He mock-saluted, then crossed back to the table, a huge smile on his hand-some face.

He sipped the coffee, and then got straight to business, without a word about the interaction with Celia. I was dying to ask about the history between them, but I didn't want to distract him from my case.

"So, from what you sent to my office, it looks like your initial request was very fair—conservative even. My recommendation is that you raise the ini-tial settlement, as well as the child support number based on his income for the current tax year. These are the figures I'd recommend."

He slid a single sheet of paper across, and I couldn't hide the shock on my face at the *much* higher figures than what the mediator had recom-mended.

"That being said, your initial request included alimony payments, but I don't think that's wise. You're young and lovely, with a little girl to raise. The likelihood of you staying single for the full amount of time you should be due alimony is slim. I'd recommend that you negotiate a number more along these lines in lieu of monthly alimony payments."

He slid a second sheet across, and I felt faint at the number of zeroes on the paper. "That seems like a lot of money. Does Carl even have that much? I never saw any bank statements with anywhere near that in them."

He steepled his fingers and looked at me over the top. "I had a feeling you were under-asking, given his threats in the monetary department. That sort of move is typically defensive, meant to scare you off from looking too deeply. So, I hired someone to do just that, and dig into what assets were there. Here's what we found." He slid a third sheet across, which listed four accounts I had no idea existed, plus a much higher value for the house than I'd expected. "We're now asking for half of everything, which is fair, given that he was still fresh out of school and earning very little when you married. Or he can pay sixty percent up front, and skip alimony. The initial request was barely a quarter of what you're entitled to, and he was stupid to fight it."

"I don't know what to say. This all sounds amazing, but he's threatened to come after Josie. There is no dollar amount that's worth losing my baby over. Can we ensure he doesn't threaten custody again?"

He sighed. "I hate to recommend a single mother take a penny less than the cheating ex owes her, but given his connections and his lack of care, we could offer him the option to terminate his parental rights. If he does that, though, you'll never receive child support again. Since he only cares about the financial haircut he's taking, the substantial sum should be motivating."

He scowled, clearly put out by Carl's behavior as much as I was. By the time we'd gotten settled in at Celia's, Josie had already stopped asking about Carl. For all the time we'd lived in the same house, he'd made no effort to truly bond with her, and in a way the two of us had always been more of a dynamic duo. Fatherhood hadn't fit him, and it showed in their lack of a relationship. "Yes, I'll gladly go without child support if that means this won't be an issue ever again. Please."

"I understand, and I'll contact his lawyer immediately to send over the new petition. I think it's best that we lead with the full ask, so he knows how much he'll be saving by terminating his rights. He might have a big bark, but we know what he really cares about." He drained the last of his coffee, and then stood. "If you have any questions or concerns, don't hesitate to call my cell."

"Thank you, Lawrence. I appreciate your help more than you can know."

He smiled. "You're welcome. I enjoy getting to squash scumbags. It's the best part of my job." He rapped his knuckles on the table jauntily and strode out, leaving me staring at three sheets of paper, pondering the future.

NINE

Hercules

The good thing about moving was that it didn't leave you much time to ponder how mad your ex would be when your lawyer more than doubled your divorce settlement request. I had been huffing and puffing, hauling boxes into the house and unpacking them one at a time for an hour, cleaning as I went. I was in a full sweat when a friendly horn beep surprised me into dropping one directly onto my foot. Biting off a swear, I hobbled to the front door and spotted a familiar white park ranger's truck out front.

Jensen stepped out and crossed the driveway to envelop me in a hug. I was thrilled that he'd been thoughtful enough to come help us move, and happy to be in his arms when I wasn't crying. I was sweating, though, and that might be worse.

"How's moving going?" he asked, as he settled in with his arm around my shoulders and looked through the open doorway to where I'd abandoned the toe-crushing box.

"Oh, it's going. I've probably moved about a third of what we have—most of it Josie's toys and books—and the list of stuff we need to get is a mile long. So, right on schedule," I joked.

"Well, I'm here, and happy to be put to work. Are there more boxes in the car?"

"A couple, and Celia is on her way with Josie and another load in the back of her SUV." I wiped my forearm across my sweaty brow, trying to be inconspicuous.

"All right. Let's get a move on, then." He waggled his eyebrows, and I groaned at the corny joke.

"No, nope, nuh-uh. Keep your puns to yourself, mister." I put my hands on his shoulders, and pointed him back towards my car.

He chuckled and headed for the back seat to grab another box. I watched him walk away for a long moment, distracted by all those muscles, then had to dart up the stairs to keep from getting caught staring.

I decided to spare my toes, and just shove the heavy box across the floor to the kitchen, since it contained the few pots and pans I still owned. It wasn't a full set by any means, but it was going to have to do for a while. Jensen trotted past me with a box like it weighed nothing, headed to Josie's room.

I was still shoving the pots and pans when he came back out, and he bent down and scooped it up, shaking his head as he deposited it effortlessly on the kitchen counter.

"Why don't you unpack some things, and I'll do the heavy lifting," he suggested. "There's not much left to bring in, unless you want to pick up another load. We can take my truck."

"That would be great, but I want to wait for Josie to get here first. She hasn't seen the house yet, and I can't wait to see her expression when she sees her new bed."

"I'm sure she'll love it." He grinned at me and whistled a tune as he headed back out to grab another box. Who was that happy about moving? Jensen, apparently.

I meandered back to Josie's room and began putting away the items in the box. It went quickly, and before long I was in a groove. Empty the box, flatten, drop on the porch, and hit the next box Jensen already had waiting. I was unloading my fourth box when I heard Jensen greet Celia and Josie, and headed for the front door to meet them.

"Who are you?" Josie's little voice asked.

"I'm Jensen, your mom's friend."

"Mama says I'm not allowed to call grown-ups by their first names," she said with a dramatic sigh as I rounded the hall and came into view. Aunt Celia gave me a happy wave and wandered past me into the kitchen to explore on her own.

"Yeah, that's a good rule. I had the same one when I was growing up. How about Mr. Jensen? Is that allowed?" He was squatted down to her level, a very serious look on his face.

"Yeah, prolly. Do you live in this house too, Mr. Jensen?" Her eyes were wide, taking in our new home.

"No, ma'am, this is all for you and your mama. Do you like it?"

"It's pretty. I like the dangly flowers." She pointed at some lovely wisteria blossoms growing along the porch. "We've never had a house with dangly flowers before. Hey, Mama! Can I see my room, pretty please?" She tucked her folded hands up under her chin imploringly.

"Absolutely. But I wonder if you can find it yourself before I get there?" I tapped my chin, knowing she'd love the challenge.

"I bet I can find it first!" She took off like a shot, peeking into all the rooms she flew past as Jensen and I trailed after her.

When she found her new bed, her ear-splitting squeal of happiness filled my heart with joy, and I knew I'd done the right thing by taking this lease. It might complicate things with Jensen, but I'd do anything for my baby girl. I stood in the doorway of her new room, and watched as she kicked off her shoes and flung herself onto the bedspread.

"Mom, it's so *pretty!*" She did a snow-angel on the covers, and then asked, "Can we stay here forever?"

My heart squeezed, and just like that, I was feeling guilty for the pain and disruption that Carl had put her through to bring us here.

"We'll see, baby girl, we'll see. But we're staying at least three whole years."

"That sounds like forever," she said happily, and I snorted. Three years probably was a long time when you were only six, so I'd count that as a win. The next time we moved, it would be on our terms, not to get out of an unstable situation.

"Have fun in your room, I'll be in the kitchen un-packing some more!"

"Okay, Mama!" She waited until I walked out of sight, but I heard her jumping on the bed. I'd let it slide just this once.

I blew out a tired breath as I walked back into the kitchen, where Celia had already taken over unpacking my sole kitchen box.

"The place is beautiful, honey. I'm so glad Leeann found it for you."

I crossed to her side and wrapped her in a grateful hug. "Thank you, Aunt Celia. None of this would have been possible without you."

"Oh, sweet girl, you've always got me on your side." She returned my hug, and then got back to business. She never did like to sit around idly. "Why don't you and Jensen run get the next load of boxes, and I'll stay here and keep unpacking with Josie."

I looked at Jensen, who was leaning against the counter waiting for instructions. He perked up at the suggestion. "Sounds good to me."

"Okay, we'll be back in a few. Tell Josie for me?"

"Absolutely," Celia agreed.

The ride to Celia's house was uneventful, but it wasn't until I was standing in front of her garage, the small pile of our belongings in boxes in front of us, that I began to regret the decision to allow Jensen to help us move. We had so little; it felt like a giant arrow pointing to another way in which my life was too complicated, too imperfect for him. He owned the house; we couldn't even afford to properly rent it. He had it fully furnished; I didn't own a scrap of furniture.

My face burned as he surveyed the boxes and finally spoke, "What goes, and what stays?"

"The cardboard ones are mine, the few rubber bins are Celia's. She has an unholy amount of Christmas decorations."

He snorted a laugh. "Isn't that backwards? Unholy Christmas?"

"Maybe, but you haven't seen how many bins there are. There are more behind my stack." I gestured to the back of the garage.

"Well then, let's get it uncovered so I can gawk properly." He started loading boxes into the truck with machine-like efficiency, and no comments on how few there were. I wasn't as quick as him, but I still helped load the truck—I had my pride, after all—and in ten minutes, we were done. His truck bed was barely half full, and there were no boxes left.

I stood there with a lump in my throat, struggling to come to grips with how much my life had changed, when he slung a sweaty arm around my shoulder.

"Wow."

Here it comes. The judgment.

"That is an unholy amount of Christmas decorations. Does she put all that up by herself?" He scratched his beard, completely unaware of my inner shame.

"I don't know. I think she pays some of the neighbor's sons to help her. It takes the full week after Thanksgiving." I tried to force some levity in my voice, but it didn't work.

"Hey, what's wrong?" His green-eyed gaze searched mine, concern wiping away his amusement over Celia's collection of Christmas decor.

"Nothing, I'm fine."

"Are you having second thoughts about moving? Did I do something wrong?" I shook my head vehemently.

"No, of course not. The house is gorgeous, you've been more than amazing, especially considering the fact that we're just friends."

He shook his head in amusement that I'd pointed that out again. "For now, maybe," he said with a cocky grin.

"How can you still want to be involved with me, Jensen? My life is a mess. I have a cheating ex, a six-year-old daughter, an entry-level job at the town restaurant, and I can't even afford to rent an apartment without my aunt's help. Can't you see that I'm no catch?" My voice cracked on the last line, and I turned away from him, leaning against the truck to hide the tears welling in my eyes. *Again.* I hated them even as they threatened to break free. I was stronger than this; I knew it.

I heard and felt him step up behind me. His solid warmth was a comfort, even without him saying a word. And he didn't, at first. Instead, he wrapped his arms around my waist in a comforting embrace and settled his chin on top of my head. And that was all. He held me close, letting me calm down. Supporting me through another meltdown without judgment.

Long moments passed, and at some point I leaned back into his comforting embrace, matching my breaths to his slow, steady ones. When I'd completely calmed, he spoke.

"When I look at you, I don't see what you see. I see a strong, fiercely independent woman. A wonderful, devoted mother who would do *anything* for her daughter. Someone who's gone through hell and back and is still swinging on the other side. You don't let anything stop you. Not an S-O-B of a cheating ex-husband, not starting over in a new town, not parenting alone, not working long hours on your feet, not financial difficulty, nothing. You are Hercules, taking hundreds of blows and staggering out on the other side, victorious. You're not a mess. You're a warrior, and I'm in awe of you."

My heart nearly stopped in my chest at his words; the beauty in how he saw me was beyond comprehension. Could he really mean that? I turned in his grip, desperate to see his eyes. When I craned my neck back to look up at him, all I saw was serene sincerity in their emerald depths.

I couldn't help myself in that moment—I flung my arms around his shoulders and laid a kiss on him fit to make a nun blush, twining my fingers into his dark chestnut hair and pulling him closer. Once I'd felt the delectable heat of his lips down to my very toes, I pulled back, and bit my bottom lip at his surprised look.

"What was that for?"

"For being you." I shrugged one shoulder, not in the mood to explain myself.

"To think I've been me every day of my whole life, and never once been kissed like that before today. You are something special, Magnolia Abbott." He reached up reverently and twined a finger through a wild curl, before gently tucking it back into place.

"You're pretty special yourself, Jensen Reed. I think I'll keep you around a while."

"I hope you do," he said as I took his hand, and he led me around to my side of the truck.

TEN

In The Attic

T he beauty of having so little to move was that by nightfall we were moved in. It took forty forevers for Josie to settle into bed, the excitement of the new house impossible to tamp down. She'd talked a mile a minute for her entire bath and every second after until I'd kissed her on the head, turned off the light, and closed her bedroom door for the night.

When I was finally in the silent, dim hallway, I sighed, and sank against the wall for just a moment, taking it all in. All day was a constant rush of things to do—move, unpack, organize, get the couch delivered, add to the mile-long list of things we needed, run to the store for basics so we'd at least have toilet paper and milk for cereal in the morning.

It had been a long, long day. Aunt Celia and Jensen were amazing, sticking it out with me until the bitter end, which was all of us eating pizza around the kitchen island on takeout napkins from Jensen's truck for dinner. Now that it was over, I finally had a few minutes to think about the momentous shift in my life this week.

I had a home that was all my own; my daughter and I were safe and secure; I had a lawyer who was going to get me a reasonable divorce settlement, while protecting my custody of Josie; and Jensen . . . well, he was a tantalizing possibility that I couldn't stop thinking about. Pushing myself away from the wall, I took a long, languorous shower before slipping into my pjs, grabbing my latest book, and propping up in the new-to-me bed.

My eyes were finally drifting closed, the words on the page running together in a blur when a noise overhead startled me to wakefulness. I froze, book clutched to my chest and eyes trained on the ceiling as I tried to figure out what was going on. A few long minutes passed, and I had just started to think that it was an odd gust of wind in the trees when it came again—a scratching, snuffling sound right above my head.

There was something up there. In the attic. Frantically, I tried to think of what to do. I certainly wasn't going up there, but maybe if I made enough noise I could scare it off. I jumped out of bed with my adrenaline pumping, and hunted for a broom.

Finally, I remembered which closet I'd stuck it into, and darted back into my room. I had to climb onto my bed to reach the ceiling, but I could still hear whatever it was moving up there. I gave the ceiling several loud jabs with the broom handle, and the thing went still, before I heard scurrying sounds heading off to the right.

"That's right, you run, sucker!" I raised the broom victoriously overhead, proud of myself for handling the critter on my own. Once the noise had stopped completely, I propped the broom against the wall next to my nightstand, and crawled back into bed, where I stared at the ceiling for nearly an hour, wide awake after the ordeal, and spotted a dent I'd left in the sheetrock with the broom handle. Ugh. I glanced at the clock and groaned to see it was after one in the morning.

Reluctantly, I picked my book back up, flipped the lamp on, and started to read again. A few chapters in, much-needed sleep finally won, and I passed out with the book on my chest.

The sounds of crying woke me, and I lurched upright in the bed. "Josie? What's wrong? Where are you?" I rubbed my tired eyes, unable to spot her in the unfamiliar room.

"Mama, I had a bad dream!" She wailed, collapsing into my lap.

"Oh, honey, it's okay. Come on, climb in with me." She kneed me in the ribs as she climbed over, and I helped her get settled in next to me under the covers. "What was the dream about?" I asked, rubbing her hair in soothing strokes.

"I don't know, Mama. Something was chasing me, and I couldn't get into the house."

"Well, nothing is here but you and me, and we're snug as can be in our new house. You're safe."

"Okay, Mama. I love you." She sighed, curling up on her side with her eyes already closed. I stroked her hair for a few more moments, until I was sure she was firmly back asleep. Laying back down, I rolled onto my side, and caught a glimpse of the clock. Three a.m. I turned off the lamp and shut my eyes, praying for sleep to claim me again quickly.

I'd barely had the thought when I heard something that froze me in place. Scratching, up in the attic. I groaned. "Not again, go rustle up your dinner somewhere else!" I whispered angrily at the unknown creature in the ceiling.

I thought about trying the broom handle again, but I didn't want to risk waking Josie. I could go lie in her bed, but she'd be even more freaked if she woke up and I was gone. No, I was stuck. I glared death daggers at the ceiling, willing my non-existent ESP to send the creature packing as the minutes ticked by.

My lunch restaurant shift the next day was rough. I hadn't been able to go back to sleep—the attic bandit snuffled until the sun came in through the windows. To top it off, it was Sunday, which was the busiest day of the week, and after I'd dropped Josie off at Celia's dressed for church, I'd barely had time for my first cup of coffee to kick in before the madness started. I was stealing sips every time I ran past my cup, but once church let out I didn't even have time for that. We were fully staffed, and even so I was nearly run off my feet.

I delivered so much fried chicken, I didn't even like the smell by the time my shift ended. I was about to take off my apron when Janie waved me over to the hostess's stand. "Hey, honey. I know your shift is up, but do you still want extra hours? The CMAs are coming in ten minutes, and it's an easy tip. Ashley called out sick—again—and I could really use your help, if you don't mind."

I forced down the bone-deep exhaustion and pulled up the sincerest smile I could muster. I couldn't let Janie down; she was like another aunt to me at this point. "Absolutely. Who are the CMAs, exactly?"

"Hmm? Oh, the Charitable Matrons of Adele. We're having a meeting to finalize the details of that charity event I told you about. It's just like the PTA table you helped your first day here." She gave a vaguely familiar-looking lady in a plumed hat a wave, then abandoned me at the hostess station so she could lead Hat-lady over to the long table reserved for large groups.

I was going to need more coffee.

The matrons of Adele may have been charitable—and festive, with most of them in feathered, brightly-colored hats—

but they weren't decisive. Two hours later, they were still arguing, and I was about ready to fall into the nearest booth, snoring. I hovered with a tea pitcher, and Janie waved for me to pull up a seat. The rest of the crowd had long-since left, so theirs was the only table still occupied in the place.

I retrieved a fresh cup of coffee and then sat wearily, trying to follow what they were arguing about.

"Yes, yes, we always do excellent food. Janie is on top of that, as always. But we need a new venue. Somewhere that's not the same old church fellowship hall. No matter how many ways we decorate it, it's still the same old place. No, we need a change of scenery, if we want a better turn out," Plume-hat-lady argued.

Dolly Blake twiddled a pearl necklace across from her, a thoughtful look on her face. "As much as I hate change, I admit that Plumeria is right. We need something more exciting. A new venue would be good, but what if we included an auction?"

Plumeria? Who named their kid that?

"Yes, but where, ladies? The fellowship hall is the only place in town that can hold as many people as we need to hit our goal and revamp the children's area of the library. It's drab, and we can do better than drab!" Another woman cast in her two cents.

"We could set up event tents," Janie suggested.

"Tents! What's festive about tents? And where?" Plumeria huffed.

"Well, I don't have a location in mind, but somewhere scenic would be best," Janie hedged.

"At the library, so people could see where their donations would be going?" Dolly supplied.

"Blech, that's a parking lot. There is nothing awe-inspiring or pocket-book-opening about a library parking lot." Dolly made a sour face. "No, we can do better, ladies."

"What about the Double F Ranch?" I suggested, surprising myself even as I said it.

All of their heads swiveled towards me, and I had the most bizarre feeling of being watched by a flock of overly coiffed owls.

"Isn't that a ways out of town?" Plumeria asked.

"Well, yes. But they've got a really pretty gazebo overlooking a lake. The field is full of flowers, too.

You'd have plenty of room to set out tents, and maybe even some fun outdoor games. You know, corn hole, giant Jenga, that sort of thing," I stammered, unnerved by the weight of all their eyes on me.

"It has potential!" Dolly declared, sharing a nod with Plumeria.

"We could do fair food, something different. Funnel cakes and smoked briskets. Beau might even be willing to smoke up a mess of turkey legs, if we bribe him."

"That could be fun, open it up to the youngsters," one of the more elderly ladies agreed.

"Well, this has been most productive. I think we can break and finalize the details after I speak with the Double F Ranch, and secure their location." Plumeria nodded to me, adjusting her hat.

Janie rose, turning to me. "Let's get the checks, and then you can head home. Thank you for staying, and the suggestion." Her warm smile made it worth it, even though my feet were leaden as we crossed to the register to start readying checks.

ELEVEN

Furry Bandit

Three nights. It had been three sleepless nights of unsuccessfully scaring off my attic invader, and I was growing desperate. Instead of taking extra hours today, when my work shift ended I was going to drag the old, rusty ladder out that I'd found in the back shed and go up there with a flashlight. I was too tired, and something had to give—either my hairy upstairs neighbor had to go, or I was going to die from lack of sleep.

I was counting down the minutes until my shift ended, leaning on the prep counter with my chin propped in my hands, when Jensen walked in for a late lunch. I was happy to see him, but also reluctant to put off my critter-scoping plans. Janie pointed him to an empty table in my section, and I met him there with my order pad.

"Hello, beautiful." He gave me the smile I was quickly growing addicted to and slid into the booth.

"Hey, yourself. Unfortunately, my shift is almost over—"

"That's perfect, want to have lunch with me? I'll buy." He gestured invitingly to the seat across from him.

"No, I can't today. I have to get home and take care of some things."

His eyebrows crinkled in, creating a confused line between them. "Is everything okay? You sound exhausted," he said, voice filled with concern.

"Well, no. There is something in the attic, and it's keeping me up. So, I'm going to haul the ladder in and see if I can do something about it."

"Wait, there's something in the attic, and you didn't call me?" He leaned forward, his frown deepening. "Magnolia, I'm your landlord. I can take care of it for you. I'll stop by as soon as I'm off work. You should get some rest."

"No, Jensen, really, I didn't tell you so you'd have to swoop in and fix it. I don't want to be one of those tenants who calls you about every little thing."

He ran a hand through his hair, and for the first time, I saw real frustration in his clenched jaw.

119

"Magnolia, have I given you the impression that you're bothering me? Have I seemed unavailable, or uninterested in helping you when you need it?"

"No, of course not."

"Then why won't you let me help you? I want to, and in this case it's my actual, contractual job to take care of the house for you. Pest control is the landlord's duty per the lease."

"Oh. Well . . ."

"I'll be by after work. Now, do you want to have lunch with me, or do you need to go home and take a nap?"

I bit my lip, torn. I wanted to spend time with him, but I was so freaking exhausted.

He reached forward and squeezed my hand. "It's okay, I can see the answer on your face. Go home and get some rest. I'll swing by later."

"Will you stay for dinner? I'll feed you," I blurted impulsively.

His eyebrows shot up in surprise. "Of course, if you're sure."

"I'm sure. If we can't have lunch, let's have dinner."

"It's a date."

"It's a date," I agreed with a flutter of nerves.

I stuck his usual order ticket in the window, cashed out for the day, and told him goodbye as

I headed out the door to get some much-needed sleep before Josie got home from school.

A two-hour nap later, I was a new woman, and anxiously anticipating Jensen's arrival. I ran to the grocery store and picked up the stuff to make a nice spaghetti dinner. I even called Celia and asked her to bring me some of her fancy garlic knots when she brought Josie, to round out the meal and make it a little more special.

Rather than pace the hallway waiting for his imminent arrival, I swept on some mascara, and spruced up my curls. Then I felt ridiculous—he'd spent all Saturday watching me sweat in my ratty work clothes while I moved . . . but, hey, maybe this image would replace the messy one from the weekend.

I'd just finished my makeup when he knocked on the front door, a tall, shiny ladder under one arm. I stepped aside to let him in, and he pressed a sweet kiss to my cheek before walking to the hallway, where the attic entrance was. He wasted no time getting it set up and climbing it to take a look with a flashlight he pulled from his back pocket. I stood there feeling useless as he disappeared into the attic.

"Oh yeah, something's been up here nosing around. The insulation's been moved."

"Yeah, it has been a busy bee," I called up through the hole.

His head appeared, his grin upside down. "Well, don't worry, I'll find out where it's getting in, and get it taken care of in no time. It's going to take a while for me to check all the corners for entry spaces, so don't feel like you have to stand there the whole time."

"Okay, well, just holler if you need something."

"Will do," he said, and disappeared again.

I meandered into the kitchen and started shaping meatballs, the sounds of his boots overhead distracting me occasionally. After a while I heard his boots on the ladder, so I washed my hands and walked around to see if he was done. If so, that was fast.

"Okay, I only found one obvious point of entry, so I am going to get that closed up. There's nothing up there now—I searched the entire attic—so, if that's its only way in, you should be sleeping in peace tonight."

"That would be amazing. Thank you, Jensen." I rested my hand on his forearm and gave it an appreciative squeeze.

"You're welcome, Magnolia. That's what I'm here for." I leaned in closer, magnetized by his selfless charm, and helpful spirit. He really was the total package, and with every interaction he drew me a bit further in. Before long, I'd be his—hook, line, and sinker—and we weren't even dating.

He leaned forward too, as drawn in as I was, when I heard Josie chattering incessantly on the walk, and then her pink sparkle boots tromp-tromp-tromping up the stairs, the stream of words never pausing. Sometimes I wondered how she even breathed. Celia murmured something to her in response, as she burst in the front door.

"Mom! I'm hooooome!" she hollered, and I heard the thud of her lunch box on the floor, followed by the shrugging and swish of her jacket landing in a heap next to it.

I stepped away from Jensen to walk around the corner and saw exactly the scene I'd envisioned, but with her curly ponytail adorably askew.

"Hey sweetheart, did you have a good day at school?" I threw the kitchen towel over my shoulder so I could give her a hug. She catapulted herself into my arms, nearly bowling me over.

"It was *the best*, Mom. There's going to be an extraganza, and everyone's invited!"

"What's an extraganza?" I asked, looking to Celia, who shrugged, just as Jensen came around the corner behind me.

"We were just trying to suss that out on the walk." She smiled and shrugged at us.

"It's fun! You know, where everyone dresses in costumes, and we celebrate spring. She called it the Spring School Extraganza, and I get to be a flower. But she didn't tell me what color. I hope I'm pink." She twirled at the thought, her skirt waving about her merrily.

"Extravaganza?" Jensen supplied.

"Yes! Extra-*ba*-ganza!" she agreed. "You're invited, too. Will you come?" She stared up at him hopefully, and he darted a glance at me for confirmation.

"Oh, honey, we won't make Jensen come. He's a very busy man." I gave her the "mom smile". The one that usually communicated "drop that right now" quite well. Today, however, it elicited a pronounced pout.

"But, Mom, Mrs. Levi said *very specifically* that we should invite our friends. Mr. Jensen is our friend, so he should come. Right, Mr. Jensen?"

"Absolutely, kiddo," he said, and ruffled her hair, not helping the crooked ponytail situation.

"See, Mom? He wants to come." She beamed at me, and Celia directed her to the kitchen.

"Let's get a snack, Jo-jo."

"Okay." They bustled off, and Celia cast me a sympathetic look over her shoulder.

Jensen and I were left standing in the foyer, and I awkwardly tried to think of a way to release him from the obligation of sitting through an elementary school's spring program. "You really don't have to come; I can tell her you're busy."

Amusement twinkled in his eyes. "I would not *dream* of disappointing a lady who's asked me to her Spring Extravaganza. My mama raised me better than that." He winked and went out to his truck, to get the attic-closing materials he needed.

I was in so, so over my head.

My spaghetti dinner was delicious, and Celia's garlic knots were a hit for both Jensen and Josie. As the meal wore on, I watched with rapt attention as Josie and Jensen continued to interact. He was amazing with her, and she had warmed up to him quicker than I'd ever seen her take to anybody. I barely had to talk, as those two kept up a chatter during the whole meal. I nibbled my second piece of bread, enjoying their silly exchange.

Josie giggled as she slurped down a long noodle, splattering sauce along the way. Then she used her forefinger and thumb to pinch the end of one, and held it aloft. "Noodle contest! I have the longest noodle!"

Jensen looped a noodle loosely around his fork and held it up next to hers. It was slightly shorter. "Ah, no. She's winning! What about you, Magnolia? Can you secure the win for Team Grown-up?" He clenched his fist, into the silly game.

Josie's eyes bored into me, waiting to see if I'd play along or scold her for playing with her food. I shook my head at their antics but fished around looking for a good-sized noodle. Finding one, I held it up.

"Ha! Mama's is shortest of all. I win, I win, I win!" She did a little dance as she slurped down her prize-winning noodle.

Jensen and I both chuckled at her enthusiasm, our eyes meeting warmly over the table.

He looked back down at Josie, who'd insisted on sitting next to him. "What do you win for having the best noodle?"

"I am *the awesomesauce*."

"Err, what?" He looked at me for clarification, but I shrugged. She was always coming up with something new.

"You know, awesome-sauce! Like, the best ever."

"Ahh, so fame and glory?"

She nodded, still dancing in her seat.

"So, what would you call not the best ever?"

She thought hard, taking the question seriously. "A pooter-head. Because they *stink*," she said, then dissolved into uproarious laughter.

I rolled my eyes with amusement, used to her brand of humor, but Jensen genuinely cracked up. He laughed so hard, tears formed at the corners of his eyes and his face turned red.

Josie grinned at me, proud of herself. "Mama, I'm full. Can I go start my bath?"

"Absolutely. Tell Mr. Jensen good night."

"'Night, Mr. Jensen!" She held up a hand for a high-five, which he gave her, then darted down the hall.

"I guess that's my cue, too. Can I wash up? This was delicious, it doesn't seem fair to leave you with the cleanup, too." He stood and pushed in his chair.

Wow. I could count on one hand the number of times Carl cleaned up the kitchen, and most of them involved me down with the stomach flu or some other ailment. "No way, it's my treat tonight," I insisted, as the sound of water starting in the tub rolled down the hall to us.

"I really don't mind, but I'll offer a raincheck if you're sure."

"I'm sure. Running off my attic intruder was plenty for one day."

He snorted. "Well, the true test will be tonight, if they find a way back in. But I don't think they will." I came around the table and walked him out to the porch.

"Josie, I'm walking Mr. Jensen out," I called down the hall and waited for her answer before shutting the door behind us. It was dark, the porch light's merry glow the only thing lighting up the evening.

There was a cool breeze, and I rubbed at the sudden goosebumps that sprang up on my arms.

"Thank you for dinner tonight. It was awesome-sauce." He winked at me.

"You're very welcome. And when did you start saying awesome-sauce?" I squinted at him.

"Hmm, about five minutes back. Seemed prudent."

I couldn't help the chuckle that broke free at that. He kept me entertained, this man. He stepped forward, and I could feel the heat bloom between us, like a flower bursting up in spring. Warm and alive—the feeling made me want to lean into him, soak it up and save it for later.

He reached up and gently ran a hand over my cheek, the touch light as a feather. His face was intent, like he was thinking deep thoughts as he looked down at my face.

"What are you thinking?" I asked.

"Mm, I'm thinking about how good your lips would feel on mine right now, but that probably wouldn't be appropriate." He glanced over my shoulder, where Josie was inside none the wiser to the grown-up feelings happening on the porch.

I sighed but didn't disagree.

"Maybe a hug, then?" He opened his arms wide, and I stepped into them gladly. Being wrapped up warm against his chest was the best thing I'd felt all day.

We stayed locked together like that for a long moment, neither of us feeling the need to speak. His steady heartbeat thudding under my ear brought a calm I struggled to find lately, and I was loath to move.

When he next spoke, it was with a chuckle in his tone. "I think we succeeded in closing up the attic."

I pulled back, confused by the sudden change of topic. "What?"

He pointed over my shoulder towards the fence, where a raccoon was perched.

"Is it just me, or does he look disgruntled?"

I snickered. "Better him than me."

"Go on, now!" Jensen raised his voice and waved at the raccoon, who ambled away lazily.

"Are you working at the diner tomorrow?"

"Yes, lunch shift. You coming by?"

He ran his thumb lightly over my lip, and nodded. That serious look was back on his face, and I wished I could read minds.

"Sweet dreams, Magnolia."

"Sweet dreams, Jensen." *You'll be the one I dream of.*

TWELVE

Charitable

The next two weeks flew by as we settled into a routine in our new home. Drop Josie off at school or Celia's in the morning; in to work where I would see Jensen most days; pick up Josie; dinner; nightly routine; and then fall into bed exhausted.

The Charitable Matrons of Adele charged ahead with their planning—thankfully not where I had to wait on them—and tonight was the night of the big gala under the stars on the Double F Ranch. Just about the whole town was going to be there, and after dropping Josie off in the morning, Ashley and I were sent straight out to the ranch to help with preparations all afternoon. While several attractive cowboys strung up twinkle lights on every available tree, we hauled chairs, helped assemble tents, and prepped the displays for the food. There was even an oversized thermometer poster displayed in the gazebo to track the night's donations for the library. By sunset when the guests began to arrive, we were tired but the little stretch of meadow by the lake looked lovely.

Janie and the rest of her posse hauled in so much delicious-smelling food I didn't think the entire Roman army would have been able to demolish it. Aunt Celia and Josie hugged me and then took seats at one of the round eight-top tables in my section, Josie gaping happily at the beautiful lights, the decorated gazebo, and all of the hubbub.

A short while later, Jensen ambled up to the soiree with one of the cowboys from earlier in tow and gave me a friendly wave before heading off to mingle. I returned it, and Ashley leaned in to whisper, "That is a fine pair of men. If me and Matthew weren't serious I'd be trying to take one of them home with me." She slicked on a cherry-tinted lip gloss and sighed at their retreating backs.

I snorted. "I have a six-year-old. The only person I'm taking home is her."

"Maybe so, but don't think we haven't all noticed your not-so-secret admirer around the restaurant.

Jensen is smitten with you, and I haven't seen him that way since his high school sweetheart left town."

A knot the size of Tennessee formed in my throat, and I had to force it down to ask, "High school sweetheart?"

"Oh, girl. I forget you're not really from around here, you fit in so well. Yeah, he was hot and heavy in love with her for years. Everyone thought they'd be married, but they were fitful. Off again, on again. Never had eyes for anyone else though. But who could blame them? You know what Jensen's like, and Adelaide, she was so pretty she won prom queen *and* Miss Effingham County her senior year."

I swallowed again, that knot stubborn as I processed her words. "So, what happened?"

"Nobody knows, really. About eight months back they broke up—again—and this time, she ran off to Virginia. There were rumors for a while, but she never turned back up. Then all of a sudden, he's sparked up like the fourth of July for a pretty little half-Puerto Rican waitress, and the tongues are wagging that he's found himself a new Adelaide to chase."

"I—" I stopped, unsure what to say. *Is that all I am?* Was I just the next pretty thing to replace his true love—Adelaide? He hadn't said a word about her, or given me any reason to think that, but . .

. I finally landed on something to say. "We're just friends, Ashley."

She rolled her eyes at my assertion, and pressed on. "Oh, now, don't go getting that worried look on your face, you'll get frown lines. He's an honest man. I don't think he'd lead you on if he still had feelings for someone else. Everyone was just surprised he took to you so fast, that's all." She shrugged, as if it were no big thing, despite every worry-inducing fact she'd just told me.

"Ashley, your table is ready for drinks," Janie called sternly from the food prep tent, and gestured to an impatient-looking group of older couples.

"It's going to be a long night," she grumbled as she grabbed up her order pad and a pitcher of sweet tea from a tray before ambling over to the table with a pasted-on smile.

I grabbed a tea pitcher too and circulated through tables topping off drinks as I pondered everything. I wasn't even divorced yet, and Jensen was clearly on the rebound from a long-term relationship, himself. Was that all we were to each other? Were we just marking time, while we recovered from the relationships we'd left behind?

The thought troubled me more than it should for someone who was *just a friend*. Deep down, I knew I'd been feeling more than that, even if I was shoving it aside right now. I carried the troubled thoughts with me, unable to pour them out as easily as sweet tea into thirsty glasses.

When I made my way around to Celia and Josie's table to take their order from the carnival-themed menu, I saw that Jensen and a few of his cowboy friends had taken seats with them. There was one empty seat, between Josie and Jensen, for me. I tried to wipe my worry off my face and focus on the excitement of the evening.

"Mama, Mama! Aunt Celia says we're having fair food for dinner. I want a corn dog! And a funnel cake! And—"

Celia patted her on the arm, interrupting her. "Give her a minute, dear. We'll get you all the delicious treats you want tonight."

"Absolutely. Tonight's a night for celebration!" I agreed, but from the look on Jensen's face, he wasn't buying my cheerful act. The dang man could read me like a book, and it was far too early in our friendship for that. I stuck to business. "What can I get everybody tonight?"

Josie rattled off her order with gusto and hand gestures showing the *size* of the strawberry-and-sugar-covered funnel cake she wanted, and then everyone else went round robin with their orders. I headed back to put it in with Janie and Beau, who was manning both a giant barrel smoker and a deep fryer.

"Boy, your turkey legs are going like gangbusters, Beau, honey," Janie said when she called out the order.

"Of course they are—what's not to like?" He waggled his eyebrows at her playfully and tugged the bottom of her apron with a pair of tongs before she swatted him away.

"Keep your eyes on the food, mister!" she scolded him, but there was no heat to it. These two were playful as newlyweds, despite nearly forty years of marriage.

God, why had I chosen so wrong, when other people got things so right on the first try? It was a sad thought, and my mood plummeted further. I made the rounds of my other two tables, and before long I was ferrying the first round of food out into the crowd. I lost myself in the work, but the thoughts were still there, dogging the back of my mind.

It made sense now, why Jensen would be so open to me—he was vulnerable from losing Adelaide.

Otherwise, why would he have bothered with my train-wreck of a life? We probably made him feel better about how many things he hadn't screwed up.

I was dropping the last dessert plate off at Josie's table when Beau and Janie walked up behind me to speak to the platoon of cowboys occupying one side.

"Y'all, we just wanted to say thank you on behalf of the Charitable Matrons for letting us take over your gorgeous property for this event," Beau started, and it finally clicked that these had to be the Ferguson brothers.

Janie cut in, "And Brent and Jensen, you two put a real dent in our goal, so thank you for that, too!"

"We feel strongly about helping the community, Mrs. Jude. That's why we started our renovation business. It just makes sense to give back when we can," the cowboy closest to Jensen said—I gathered he was Brent.

"Well, Adele is lucky to have you all," Beau concluded, before leading Janie off to do the rounds, and I saw other women from the CMAs doing the same—circulating and thanking people for their donations.

Before I could escape to the next table, Jensen called out to me. "Magnolia, wait! Now that things are slowing down a bit, I'd like to introduce you to some of the Ferguson brothers. This is Brent, my business partner and the man who helped me renovate your house."

The steely-eyed cowboy waved. "Are you liking Huckleberry House? It's a real beauty."

"It is gorgeous. Your work is impeccable," I said, making a point to include them both in the praise.

He nodded, and Jensen continued around the table, making introductions of the other three. After we'd all exchanged pleasantries, I bustled off to look busy in the server's area. I was worn out and struggling to keep up the cheer.

It wasn't five minutes before Jensen found me. He was devastatingly handsome, with his hands tucked into his pockets and his hair ruffled by the evening breeze. "Magnolia, do you have a few minutes to take a walk with me?"

Ashley answered for me, "She absolutely does. I've got everything covered here." She gave me a firm shove forward, and when I scowled pointedly over my shoulder at her, pretended she was too busy to notice.

I stepped from under the tent and walked alongside him around the perimeter of the area, our steps lit by nothing but the moon and twinkle lights. It was beautiful, and I wished I could enjoy it instead of torturing myself with insecurity.

We walked in silence for a few minutes before he spoke, his voice gentle, "It seems like something is bothering you tonight, Magnolia. Do you want to talk about it?"

I shrugged, not wanting to admit it. It felt petty, after all he'd done for us. "It's silly, nothing to worry about."

"If it worries you, it isn't silly to me," he argued.

I stumbled over the words, trying to figure out how to explain it without embarrassment. "Ashley mentioned that you used to have a long-term girl-friend, and that you recently broke up. I just got worried that we were both trying to rebound, or that maybe you still have feelings for someone who's gone."

He nodded, not interrupting me as we continued our walk under the lights. "I can see how that would worry you, but things were never smooth sailing with Adelaide, my ex. I know there was a lot of talk around town about the two of us, which is probably what Ashley told you. We cared for each other, but we weren't compatible in the end. And Magnolia, I hope that you know I'd never treat you as just a rebound. I have feelings for you, real feelings. For you, and Josie, too. She's a little firecracker, that girl." He chuckled, and then grew serious. "Do you still have feelings for your husband, that I should be worried about?"

I blew out a frustrated breath. It was a fair question. "Sure, if you count anger, hurt, embarrassment, and frustration. Carl and I . . . we weren't in love anymore, not for a long time. Looking back, I wonder if we ever really were, or if I was just swept up in what I thought was love from him. I was so young, and so eager to find someone who looked at me the way my parents looked at each other. It was easy to believe that he and I could have that, in time." I twirled an errant curl absently, stuck in the painful memories of the hopeful girl I used to be. "But we didn't. The very beginning was the peak, and after that we drifted further and further apart. When Josie came along, it was like I put that problem on a shelf, and focused on her. I'm not saying that's right, but he was so absent, even when he was with us . . . She has always been warm, and full of light. Firecracker is a good description."

We smiled at each other then, bonding over my feisty girl.

"It takes two to break a marriage. It's not just your fault. He can't have been that devoted to the relationship's success, given how things ended."

With him in the arms of another woman. "It's true. Is it bad that it still stings, even if I'm happier now? We're more settled and more content now without him, and Josie rarely ever brings him up. It's like we've just erased him, in a way. But something about what he did . . ."

He reaches over and takes my hand in his, twining his warm fingers with mine. "Of course it stings. You're human, and it was a betrayal. But it's good that you've found your footing. I think you two can flourish here and put it behind you; you've already started putting down new roots."

"I think so too, if I can just make it through the divorce itself. Lawrence is trying to get us a court date in the next few weeks."

"Are you nervous, or ready to get it over with?"

"Both. I want to be done with it, be free. But, there's a small part of me that's nervous that he'll try to take custody of Josie. He threatened it, even though I don't think he'd really want to be responsible for her." I shook my head, anger rising. "I don't even care about the money, but the fact he'd try to use my baby as a bargaining chip—it just makes me want to strangle him."

"You and me both." He gave my fingers a supportive squeeze, and it occured to me that we were in plain sight of all the townspeople, walking and holding hands for all to see. I felt a flash of concern over what they would think, but intentionally pushed it away. I was a grown woman, and we weren't doing anything inappropriate.

"Is that all that was bothering you?" he asked when we're almost back around the clearing.

I hesitated, unsure if I should tell him what else was on my mind, but also wanting to be honest with him. "Jensen, I'm just not sure I'm good for you. We've been over my complications, but the other side of the coin is just as important. You have your life together. You've got a good job, a successful side business, you're respected in town, and you've obviously got money and connections. I'm not sure why you'd want to be with me, when our lives are so different."

He stopped dead still; as he turned to face me a particularly exuberant light overhead caused his forest green eyes to sparkle. "You're not seeing yourself clearly, still, so let me paint you a picture, Mags."

The nickname on his gorgeous lips made me catch my breath.

"I've got my life together, sure. I don't have financial trouble, and I enjoy my work. At night, when I go home, my house is empty. Cold, even. Don't get me wrong, it's a nice house, but I've never felt more at home than when I had spaghetti dinner with you and Josie, making silly jokes, and imagining kissing you right over the table. Lunch with you at Jude's brightens my days, even if it's just a passing comment. Who cares that I have my life together if I'm alone, with no one to share it with?" He paused, cupping my cheek in his palm, like I was made of china. "You're like the sun, where my sky was just empty before. As mad as I am at your ex for hurting you, I'm counting my blessings every dadgum day that it means you're here with me, where I can bask in your light."

I leaned into his palm, feeling the calluses of his hard work scrape deliciously against my skin. What did you even say to that sort of declaration? It felt like my heart was going to explode, as I stared into his eyes.

"Can you promise me one thing?" he continued, his tone soft as velvet.

"What?"

"Don't put yourself down anymore. If you're not sure of how much you're worth, I'll remind you."

"Thank you."

"Always, Magnolia," he murmured, pressing a soft kiss against my temple.

THIRTEEN

Crisis Mode

I woke the next morning in the warm afterglow of the conversation I'd shared with Jensen. Couple that with the unusual weekend day off, and the fact that Josie was still worn out and sleeping in, and it was shaping up to be a glorious Sunday morning. I took a luxurious shower, taking advantage of the rare unhurried day. When I escaped the steamy bathroom in my towel to cool off and dress, my phone had a missed call and a voicemail.

Assuming it was Celia or Jensen, I tapped the voicemail to play it without checking the contact. Carl's voice bathed me in horror, instead.

"Either you're stupid, or you don't care about Josie's custody as much as you act like you do. I gave you very clear instructions. Drop the financial requests, keep the kid. Instead, you have the gall to hire a lawyer and try to *raise* the settlement amount, after you were a mediocre wife at best? If this is how you repay my generosity over the years, get ready. My lawyer is going to make sure you don't get a dime, and you don't see our daughter ever again. This is not how it's going to go down, Magnolia." He snarled my name like a curse, and my hand shook when I dropped the phone, which missed the side table and fell to the floor with a clatter.

I clutched the towel tightly around my chest and sank down to the edge of the bed, suddenly ice cold when I'd just been flushed from the shower. He was really going to try to take Josie, and it was all my fault. I should have insisted Lawrence back off, write a lesser settlement, and get this over with. He'd sounded so confident that I wanted to believe it would all be okay. But this was the furthest from okay I could imagine.

I reached down, and picked up the phone with lifeless fingers, willing them to work so I could make a phone call. "Jensen? Can you come over?"

His voice was sharp, instantly on alert. "What's wrong? Are you okay?"

"No, I'm not. Just, please come."

"On my way. I'm already getting in the truck."

I managed to get myself dressed and get Josie in front of a cartoon with a bowl of cereal by the time he arrived. I waited on the front porch steps, head in my hands until I heard him pull up the driveway. As soon as he stepped down from the truck, I lost it, tears streaming down my face in a rush. He jogged over to me and sank onto the step at my side.

He wrapped me up in his arms and whispered soothing words as he rubbed my back. "It's going to be okay. I'm here, Magnolia. What happened? What's wrong?"

Unable to explain myself, I pressed play on the voicemail and passed him the phone. I leaned into his shoulder and looked up to watch disbelief and rage war on his face when the voicemail ended.

"That sorry excuse for a man. I cannot believe he said any of that to you, about his own daughter. It makes me want to drive over there and beat some sense into his sorry hide." He seethed, but then seemed to realize he had to rein it in for my sake. "Have you called the lawyer?"

I shook my head. "I just called you. I don't know what to do, Jensen. I'm scared. I want to just drop the whole thing and let him keep everything if he'll sign over his rights to Josie. I don't ever want to feel like this again."

"Hey, listen to me. No judge is going to give that man your daughter, when they sit down and look at the situation. Let's call Lawrence and give him an update. He'll know what to do, but you aren't going to let him scare you into submission. I'm here, and we're going to fix this. Do you want me to call him, or do you?"

"You can," I said, the words pitifully small. The idea of Carl taking Josie and keeping her for me had sent me into a full-blown panic, and I wasn't entirely out of it yet, even though Jensen's strength was anchoring me.

He didn't waste time; he called Lawrence up, updated him in a few terse lines, then put the phone on speaker so I could hear as well.

"Maggie, can you hear me?"

"Yes, Lawrence. I'm sorry to bother you on a Sunday."

"Don't apologize, I'm on your side. Listen to me—we are going to get through this, and there is no chance in hell a judge is going to take your baby away from you and throw away the key. You are a

147

great mother, and we have everything we need to prove it. I want you to send me that voicemail, right now. Do not respond to him in any way, let him think he's got you running scared. I'm going to use that message to get the hearing moved up, and let's get this thing settled and behind us. Are you okay with that?"

"Yes, I want this to be over. But Lawrence . . . I'm scared. I don't want anything more than I want Josie with me. If he—" My voice cracked, and I couldn't continue. Jensen squeezed my shoulders, and I leaned my head onto his bicep.

"Do you trust me, Maggie?" Lawrence asked.

"Yes, I do."

"Good. Then trust this: we are going to win this fight. I know he's not playing fair, and I know he's being a bully. But that's all the more reason this fight matters. He doesn't deserve to get away with this, and we aren't going to let him. Now, I don't think you should be alone with this. Do you have someone who can stay with you, or who you can spend a few days with? The best thing to do in these situations is to have your support network close."

"I'll stay. I don't mind," Jensen said immediately.

"You don't have to, we could go back to Celia's," I protested. Here I was, disrupting his life again with my mess. Guilt flooded me at the whole situation. I hadn't asked what he was doing, or if he was busy. I'd only been wrapped up in my own needs and snatched him to me like an over-tight bungee cord.

"Absolutely not. If you'd feel more comfortable with her, I'll just stay until she gets here. But I'm more than happy to camp on your couch until this mess is dealt with."

"Sounds like you've got it all sorted, then," Lawrence drawled. "I'll let you go and get my people on this immediately. Send me that message; he's going to regret those words when we play them for the judge in court, I promise."

He hung up, and I let out a shaky breath. I was so ready for this to all be over.

"There, he's got a plan, and you don't have to worry." Jensen ran a hand over my curls, soothing me against his shoulder.

I nodded, but still couldn't speak. The fear had started to subside, and anger was trying to erupt in its place.

"What are you thinking, Magnolia? You're too quiet." His voice was still calm, soothing me like a wounded animal.

"It was ten years of marriage, albeit a mediocre one, and this is how he treats us. Me like I'm disposable, and Josie like a bargaining chip. As if that's all we were to him, marking time until he threw us aside for the next hot thing to trot past." My words were bitter, the anger winning out by the end.

"He's stupid, that's for sure," Jensen muttered.

His frank assessment drew a laugh out of me, breaking the hot wall of anger in a sudden burst. He chuckled too and leaned down to press a kiss to my forehead. It was a small thing, but it reminded me that Josie was inside, unaware of all the drama that had occurred in such a short stretch of Sunday morning. I pulled back, creating some space between us. The glance over my shoulder clued Jensen in, and he stood, giving me some space.

"So, do you want me to stay, or do you want to call Celia? I won't be offended, either way."

"I'd hate to make you sleep on the couch, it doesn't seem right. You've already done way, way too much for us, Jensen. Really."

He waved a hand dismissively. "Magnolia, I don't mind a bit. I've slept in worse places, for less of a reason."

I bit my lip, indecisive. The idea of having him here until this mess was over was so tempting, and it would be easy to lose myself in him. I could let him take over—I could be the one who hides while the men duke it out on her behalf. Is that who I wanted to be, though? "I appreciate the offer, Jensen, but I am okay now. The crisis is under control, and all we'll be doing is waiting for a court date. You can spend the day with us if you want, though." There, calm and reasonable—standing on my own two feet.

"Absolutely." He gave me an affable smile, but I saw a shadow of disappointment on his face that I wanted to erase.

I reached out my hand for his, and he stepped forward to lace his fingers with mine. I gave our hands a gentle swing before finally thinking of what to say. "I appreciate you so much, Jensen. This is something that I can handle, though," I said in my most confident tone. "I need to learn to do things for myself, stand on my own two feet. I have to get stronger if I'm going to make a life for us on my own."

"I'm pretty sure you're strong enough to bench press a train car if you wanted. But I respect that. You're an independent woman; that's one of the many things I love about you." His mouth curled up at the corner, the disappointment disappearing.

My heart fluttered in my chest at his words. That was dangerously close to saying he loved me . . . but surely he couldn't so soon, right?

The front door banged open, and Josie's bare feet pattered onto the porch, saving me from responding. "Mr. Jensen! I'm so glad you're here. Have you ever seen the Mutant Turtle Ninjas? They are soooo cool. One of them has two swords, but Mama says they're named after painters. That seems like a weird thing because they live underground and fight bad guys."

He grinned a mile wide, and stepped onto the porch as he answered, "I love the Ninja Turtles. Which one's your favorite?"

She reached up and snagged his hand, hauling him into the living room without a second thought. "I like the purple one. I wish there was a girl turtle, though. They should make her pink, and she would be my favorite."

"True, there should be a girl. What would you call her?"

There was a long pause. "Josie, duh."

I chuckled as I hauled myself off the front step, trailing them into the house for my own bowl of cereal and some *Mutant Turtle Ninjas*.

Fourteen

The Big D

M onday came bright and early, along with a breakfast shift at the restaurant. I dropped a bleary-eyed and pajama-clad Josie with Celia since it was too early to take her to school. I zoned in on the morning rush, letting the customers and the hopping energy keep my mind off of the divorce business. It was a welcome relief—by the time Jensen strode in for his lunch with a smile and a bouquet of flowers, I was actually in a pretty good mood.

Janie beat me to the table, where I found her oohing and ahhing over the flowers.

"My, my, look at you two," she said with a sigh. "Your shift is almost over, why don't you two have lunch? I'll bring you something special, and something to put the flowers in. That peony will wilt if it's left too long. And are those ranunculus? Darling."

Jensen seemed amenable to the idea and Janie had that glittering look of happiness in her eyes, so why not? "Sounds great. Let me just go hang my apron up."

When I settled back into the booth with him a few short minutes later, he passed me the bouquet.

There was a single line on the card, in a messy hand. "For the prettiest Magnolia to ever bloom."

I couldn't help a shy smile at the words. "Thank you, Jensen. They're gorgeous. What's the occasion?"

He shook his head. "No occasion. I just wanted to get them for you."

"You are spoiling me, Jensen Reed. Absolutely spoiling me." I leaned in to sniff the bouquet, the mix of different flowers creating a delicate perfume.

"You're infinitely worth spoiling, Magnolia Abbott."

Janie brought out drinks for us herself, and, a short time later, delicious plates of the pot roast special. We were tucking into the meal, chatting about his progress on the duck conservation project and Josie's latest exploits at school when my phone buzzed in my pocket. I checked it quickly in case it was Josie's school, since everyone else knew I was working. It wasn't the school though, it was Lawrence. He'd sent me a text.

Lawrence Jude: Court Friday at 10:15.

He was a man of few words, apparently. I set the phone down next to my silverware, trying not to fall into worry about what we'd hear on Friday. It was good that it was soon, but bad that I had four days to worry.

"What's wrong?" Jensen asked, immediately picking up on my changed mood.

"Lawrence got us a hearing Friday. This . . . it's finally going to be over."

"That's good, right?" He raised an eyebrow, his quizzical expression asking if I was having cold feet about the divorce.

"It is, yes. It's just . . . there's so many aspects to it. I feel relieved at the idea of it being behind me, but also fear of what Carl might try to pull. Then there's wariness that something we don't expect will happen. Also, I'm still hurt that this whole thing has happened at all. It's the end of a decade of my life, and I'm not sure if I'm sad it ended, or sad I wasted so much time on a man who didn't really love me." I snapped my mouth closed to stop the rambling and tried to ignore the rising blush I could feel on my

155

neck. What was it about Jensen that always made me say too much—heck, *feel* too much?

He reached across the table for my hand and ran his thumb over my knuckles. The touch was small, but tender. "It's going to be okay, Mags. One way or another, it's going to be okay."

I sighed and turned my hand over to link up with his. I shouldn't encourage all the physical contact, since I was the one constantly insisting we couldn't date. But he anchored me in such a real way, it was hard to resist. A little thrill shot through me at the realization that after Friday, I wouldn't have to resist, if I didn't want to. I'd be divorced—so, one complication down. That's what we'd been waiting on to date, right?

We finished our meals with our fingertips linked, but my brain had a whole slew of new emotions to fixate on: excitement, interest, and, most dangerous of all, hope.

Time passed strangely between when I got the message with the court date and Friday when I actually arrived at the courthouse. It was like I couldn't pin down any moment, any emotion, before I'd cycle to a new one. Worry, stress, fear, and fierce protectiveness over Josie were the most frequent, with little bursts of hope or happiness. As I sat in my car waiting to walk in—alone, because it was a teacher planning day, so Celia had to stay with Josie—dread was beating all the others by a mile.

I didn't want to see Carl. I didn't want to hear the lawyers coldly discussing our fates, Josie's fate, as if they were reading the Sunday paper. I didn't want to feel like the last ten years of my life had boiled down to a single hour, a single decision by a judge I'd never met before.

Yet here I was. I took a few deep breaths to steel my nerves, and stepped out of the car. I kept my eyes down, tracing the damp pavement as I approached the steps where I was supposed to meet Lawrence before we went in for the trial. He'd talked me through everything yesterday, so I knew his plan was a good one. Still, though, the dread just wouldn't leave.

I ascended the steps and glanced around furtively, but there was no sign of Lawrence yet. I was fifteen minutes early, so he'd be here soon. Trying to find some inner calm, I leaned back against one of the huge columns out front of the courthouse and closed my eyes. There was a breeze today, and the

lingering damp from last night's rain made everything smell fresh and clean, like it was brand new.

*After today, I'll have a fresh start, too. Just me and
Josie.*

Settled by the thought, I sucked in one more lungful and opened my eyes, once again scanning the
parking lot for Lawrence. Instead, I spotted a familiar park ranger's uniform, and traced it up to the
most alluring face I'd ever seen, where I got caught
in his liquid green gaze.

"Jensen, what are you doing here?"

He took the courthouse steps two at a time, and
stopped in front of me, an uncertain look on his face.
"I know it's a big day, and if you want me to leave, I'll
hug you and be on my way. But I thought you could
use a friendly face in there." He nodded towards
the imposing double doors. "Celia called last night
and let me know she wouldn't be able to come with
you, and it seemed like she thought you'd appreciate
some support. I took a leap."

"Jensen, that's . . ." I trailed off, unsure of what to
say. As much as I appreciated the thought, the idea
of him watching my marriage dissolve was humili-
ating. "It's really sweet, but—"

"Say no more, I'll be on my way. Good luck in there
and call me later if you want to talk." He gave me

a nod, tucked his hands into his front pockets, and turned to descend the steps.

He looked sad, and I second-guessed my hesitation. He wanted to support me, even though he knew what was coming. Was I too stubborn to let him? Could I be strong, and still let him in, or did I have to be alone?

"Jensen, wait!" I hurried down after him, meeting him at the bottom. "Stay. You're right, I don't want to be alone. I appreciate you coming all this way." I reached up a hand and brushed his arm lightly.

"Are you sure? You're entitled to your privacy, if that's what you'd prefer." He searched my face, looking for signs that I wanted him to go.

"I'm sure. Come on." I gestured back to the top of the stairs, and we ambled up together where we waited in tense silence until Lawrence arrived.

"Good morning, Maggie, Jensen!" Lawrence's voice was a deep boom rolling across the courthouse steps, and I took comfort in his commanding presence.

We both returned the greeting, and he ushered us inside and down a few hallways until we were outside our room.

"How are we feeling this morning?" he asked with an easy smile.

"Nervous," I admitted.

Jensen wrapped his arm around my shoulders and gave me a squeeze, which I leaned into.

"That is understandable, Maggie. But we've got a solid plan and we're going to wrap this up today in yours and Josie's favor." He held my gaze, as if he could will his confidence into me.

A noise at the end of the hallway pulled our attention, and my stomach gave a nervous gurgle at the sight of Carl. He was decked out in his best suit with his hair slicked back and walking next to the slimiest lawyer I'd ever laid eyes on.

Jensen whispered a question in my ear, "Is that him?"

I nodded, unable to form words seeing as how my throat had closed up with rage. This was the man who'd vowed before God to love, honor, and cherish me, and yet still thought it was okay to cheat, kick me out, and threaten to take away custody of our daughter. It was the first time I'd seen him since he'd turned from distant to nastiness, and I was surprised by my desire to jab him in the eye with my high heel. It might not solve anything, but the image was cathartic.

"Well, well, looks like we're all ready to get this mess straightened out," his lawyer said as he leaned against the wall across from us. He had a painted-on smile, but his eyes were cold enough to freeze a

Georgia summer as he appraised me, and then gave a pointed look to Jensen's arm still wrapped around my shoulders. I stiffened, but Jensen didn't remove his arm. He gave me a little squeeze and stared down the lawyer with me.

Carl took his position next to the lawyer, and a look of disgust painted his face as he took in Jensen. "Really, Maggie? Rolling up to your divorce hearing with a boyfriend in tow?" He snorted and eyed Jensen's work uniform critically. "And a step down, at that. Desperation doesn't look good on you."

Jensen ignored the jab to himself, but as soon as Carl insulted me, he stood. Crossing the space to stand directly in front of Carl, Jensen towered over him by at least four inches. He spoke in a slow drawl, "Carl, I'd recommend you keep all comments towards the lady civil. In case you've forgotten, she's the mother of your child, and even if you don't have two brain cells to rub together and see what a catch she is, you should at least remember that you owe her some respect. Otherwise, you and I can step outside and have a chat about how we speak to ladies around these parts."

Awe filled me at the sight of Jensen putting Carl in his place without lifting a finger or even raising his voice. He was glorious in his righteous indignation, and I'd never more wanted to plant a kiss on him than I did in that moment, watching him toe to toe with my scumbag of an ex.

Carl glowered at his chin, unwilling to meet his eyes. Deep down, he knew Jensen was right, but it must have rankled to see me—who'd he'd paid so little regard to—already sitting next to a better man. "Apologies, Magnolia. I'm just surprised by some of your choices."

I scoffed. "You don't get to judge my choices after what you've done, Carl. Mind your own business."

We were saved from further squabbling by the court's officer, who called us into the courtroom.

Lawrence hooked my elbow and led me to our seats up front by the judge without a word. He exuded calm confidence as he deposited me in the proper place behind our table and gestured to the first row behind us for Jensen. He nodded and picked the seat just behind and to the left of me, where I could still see him from the corner of my eye. As I took my seat, a silent spike of fear shot from my toes. This was it. For better or worse, this was happening. I closed my eyes, and drew in a slow breath through my nose, trying to find a sense of calm. I didn't want to do this while I was a panicked mess. When I opened my eyes again, Jensen looked into them, a bulwark of calm support.

I felt myself settle, and he gave me a reassuring nod. I faced forward and noted a woman sitting behind an oddly tiny typewriter, looking bored.

"All rise!" the officer intoned, and we did, as the judge walked in.

He was in his late forties or early fifties, gray spreading from his temples and a stern mien. He nodded at both tables and took his seat. He flipped open a folder, quickly reviewing the case details.

"This seems straightforward enough, aside from the custody discrepancy. What's the issue?" He looked from Lawrence to Mr. Slimeball, who jumped forward around the table to cut in, intent on getting the first word.

"Your honor, my client has objections to the financial requests submitted on Mrs. Abbott's behalf. We feel that her financial situation doesn't show that she can fully support Josie, their daughter, and that custody should be removed immediately, and returned to my client."

There it was, straight for the jugular. Was he really going to try and take her, even though he didn't want her? My pulse raced, and I felt weighted to my seat by a two-ton elephant.

He carried on pacing as he spoke, uncaring of my sudden paralysis. "Additionally, we have provided an alternative financial settlement which we feel is more appropriate, given each of their work histories throughout the term of the marriage. As you will see from the provided documents, Mr. Abbott is a career man, with a strong history of providing for his family, and has been very successful at climbing the ladder."

The judge flipped a few pages until he found the documents in question. "I see." He scanned the pages, no change in facial expression.

Did he agree with the awful lawyer? Was he going to think I was just a greedy, lazy woman? My eyes flew to Lawrence, who hadn't moved a muscle, and still sat next to me oozing confidence. There was even a hint of a curl at the corner of his mouth, as if he was *enjoying* this, which baffled me.

"I will review these before I make my decision." He looked to our table, and Lawrence finally moved. He rose slowly, as if we had all the time in the world and leaned his hip against the side of the table. The polar opposite of the frenetic slimeball, and I started to understand his method.

"Your Honor, if you'll allow me, I'd like to paint you a picture. You see, my client has been a devoted wife and mother for just over ten years. So devoted, in fact, that she dedicated her life to caring for hers and Mr. Abbott's home, and the raising of their lovely daughter, Josie." He leaned over to his own folder on the table, where he pulled out Josie's latest school picture and walked it over to place in front of the judge. He put his hands in his front pockets as he slowly walked back, allowing the silence to grow until he was once again facing the judge.

I was on the edge of my seat, waiting to hear what he'd say next.

"It was a true shock to her, when, despite her many years of devotion and care, Mr. Abbott came home from his *prestigious* job one day," he said with disdain, "and told her it was over. He'd found a new woman, in fact. Stacy, I believe her name is?" He glanced over at Carl as if for confirmation. He was red-faced but silent, so Lawrence continued. "That's not important. What *is* important, is that he also asked Maggie and Josie to vacate the premises, giving them less than seventy-two hours to do so. In fact, he promised my client that should she take Josie and be gone in the timeframe he provided, he would not ask for custody or visitation. Caring most of all for the wellbeing of her child, Magnolia packed up and took them out of there the very next day. She left with almost nothing, besides clothing and toys, not even taking a piece of furniture from the home which she'd maintained and decorated."

He tapped idly on the table, once again drawing out a pause that made me hold my breath. "Now, this doesn't exactly paint a picture of a loving and devoted father, but I'm afraid it gets worse," he said sincerely. "Maggie worked with a mediator, and put in a very low request for financial support, which you'll see I've included as exhibit A. Despite the fact that this is her due, as most courts and the entire great state of Georgia would agree, Mr. Abbott did not take kindly to the request, and refused. You see, he wanted to walk away scot-free, shucking off his commitments like yesterday's dirty socks."

"Objection, your honor!" Carl's lawyer leapt to his feet angrily.

"Apologies, I just want to paint the full picture." Lawrence gave a hand raise of acknowledgement. "Anyways, where was I? Oh, yes. Failed mediation. Now, Mrs. Abbott came to me by way of a family friend, asking for help to reach an agreeable settlement and retain custody of Josie. Now, that struck me as odd. He'd given up custody of the child. Why would she fear he'd then take it back?" He scratched his chin slowly, deliberately.

"You see, Mr. Abbott had implied that he would take Josie back if she couldn't find a way to support her wholly alone, with no further help from him. When she came to me, she was terrified. Her initial request was that I put together an agreement wherein she would meet his demands and retain sole custody of her daughter. This raised my suspicions, and I had one of my staff members do some digging into the familial assets, to ascertain the best way forward. If you look to exhibit B, you'll see the results of that inquiry. Not only was there money that Maggie was unaware of—making her initial request substantially too small—but we found that he'd opened accounts without her knowledge and begun squirreling money away two years prior to his infidelity. Or, at least, the *announcement* of it."

My jaw dropped. Carl had been planning this for *two years*? How long had he been cheating? Rage bubbled up again, and I looked accusingly over at Carl. He was redder than a tomato, gritting his teeth. So, it was true. Every word.

"Now, I advised my client to put together a fairer request, which you have in front of you as well, hoping this would be the end of it. Unfortunately, it was not. He pulled a slim black device from his pocket, laid it onto the table, and pressed a button.

Carl's voice came out, crystal clear and oozing hatred like pus. "Either you're stupid, or you don't care about Josie's custody as much as you act like you do. I gave you very clear instructions. Drop the financial requests, keep the kid. Instead, you have the gall to hire a lawyer and try to *raise* the settlement amount, after you were a mediocre wife at best?"

167

The court reporter gasped at her tiny keyboard, affronted on my behalf, and the judge's eyebrows flew upward as the vicious recording continued to play. My cheeks burned, humiliated at having to share Carl's disdain with even more people. The message ended with a soft click, and I looked down at my lap, tears prickling the backs of my eyes.

Before any could escape, a warm hand gripped my shoulder, and I looked up to see Jensen, leaning forward, lending me his strength. I let out a shuddering breath and tried to push away the shame and disgust I felt. I wasn't in the wrong, and I couldn't take responsibility for Carl's abominable behavior.

"As you can see, he not only threatens my client, his own wife, but tries to use their daughter as a bargaining chip. That is why, your honor, we've provided exhibit C."

He waits for the judge to flip another page, and recognition to show on his features.

"Exhibit C provides a possible amended financial agreement, in exchange for Mr. Abbott severing his parental rights, and giving up all shared custody or visitation of Josie Abbott, their daughter. I personally feel this request is too low, but Mrs. Abbott insisted that the primary directive was to retain Josie's custody, no matter the financial cost to her future."

After he finished addressing the judge, he slid a copy of exhibit C from his folder and slid it onto the table in front of Carl's lawyer, who quickly compared the numbers and slid it to Carl.

I held my breath, unable to look away as they hunched together whispering, and Carl's finger jabbed angrily at something. After a heated minute, they straightened, and Mr. Slimeball stood again.

"Your Honor, my client is amenable to this request with the exception of line twelve."

"Including the severing of parental rights?"

He nodded once, sharply. I peeked over at Lawrence's folder and saw that line twelve was my half of the home equity, the only request we'd maintained at half. I swallowed hard. Without that money, we would struggle to afford our own house, or to try to change careers without more help from Celia. Lawrence didn't look my way, just watched the judge with unwavering interest. He already knew I'd say yes, if it meant Carl couldn't take Josie, not now, not ever.

"I'll take that under advisement." The judge stood, swept up the folder. "Court is now adjourned for recess," he said and walked back out the door he came through.

Lawrence gestured for me and Jensen to follow him, and we walked back out into the hall. Carl and his lawyer stayed put.

My hands shook as the courtroom door closed behind us and I knotted my fingers together to try and stop it.

Jensen stood behind me, chafing my arms lightly with his hands.

"That went very well." Lawrence said, holding my gaze. "I know it was hard to sit through, but you did well. This is almost over, Maggie. I have a good feeling." His smile was calm and self-assured, and I tried to share his courage.

"Can I get you some coffee?" Jensen asked.

"That sounds great."

"Let's all walk," Lawrence agreed. "We have a few minutes while the judge deliberates."

The short field trip to the cart and the familiar routine of doctoring up my coffee steadied me, and by the time we made it back to the courtroom, they were ready for us.

"That was fast," I murmured as we walked in, settling straight back into our seats.

"Usually is, when it's an easy decision." Lawrence smiled at me, as if he already knew the outcome, then leaned back in his chair, crossing one ankle over his knee in a relaxed position.

On the other hand, I was perched lightly on the edge of my seat, knee bouncing with nerves.

"All rise!" The call came again, and I surged to my feet, eyes trained on the judge as if I could tell by his facial expression what he'd decided.

He made his way back to his seat and settled in. We all followed suit, silence falling over the courtroom in anticipation of his ruling.

He didn't waste any time. "The court feels that one party has demonstrated significantly more ability to care for the needs and wellbeing of the child, Josie Abbott. Given the opinions and information shared here today, I can confidently say that we will be moving forward with the severing of Mr. Abbott's parental rights, and awarding sole custody to her mother, Mrs. Abbott. This seems to be in line with the wishes of both parents, as well as the child's best interest. Now, in regards to the financial settlement—"

My breath seized in my lungs at those words, and I nearly choked trying to keep in a relieved sob. All the blood rushed to my ears, and I didn't hear another word he said besides that Josie was mine. For good, for keeps, and with no interference from Carl from here on out. I'd be a blessed pauper if I had nothing more than that.

I glanced back at Jensen and happiness shone in his eyes. Our gazes locked for a long moment, and then he pointed back up front towards the judge. I faced back to the front and tried to focus on the words the judge was still saying.

"—It is the court's belief that while a spouse may strongly desire to shirk his or her responsibilities, that does not make it their legal or moral right. All of that being said, I have granted the primary request from Mrs. Abbott as written, the only exception being child support, since that cannot be awarded with the severing of parental rights."

"You have got to be kidding me!" Carl shouted, and the judge turned to glare at him while his lawyer fervently tried to shut him up.

"Mr. Abbott. I understand that this is not the outcome you were hoping for. However, I would like to remind you that you were the one who chose to dissolve this marriage and leave your wife and child homeless. Your behavior has been callous at best, and reprehensible at worst. Frankly, the sight of you offends me. If you keep up your complaints, I will happily hold you in contempt." He stared Carl down, and for the first time he allowed his disgust with Carl to show on his expression.

Carl clammed up, but his fury was palpable.

"The court is adjourned," the judge said as he banged the gavel.

"What does that mean, Lawrence? Which request was primary? The one I did with the mediator?"

Lawrence leaned forward, and held both my hands in his, joy on his face as he looked me in the eyes. "Honey, you got it all. The higher request I put in, less the child support. And he terminated parental rights."

My mouth gaped open, and I couldn't think of a word to say. Not one single word. Instead, I threw my arms around Lawrence and squeezed him so hard he couldn't breathe.

He chuckled and patted me on the back until I released him to swipe at happy tears. "Lawrence, I can never repay you for the gift you've given me. But you've earned every *penny* of your fee, and thanks to you, I can actually afford to pay it, once I get my settlement. Are you going to send me an invoice?"

"Darlin' seeing that smug bastard's face turn red when the judge ripped him a new one was all the payment I need. I just love tickin' off cheaters. It's a rare pleasure when you get a front-row seat to someone being dealt *exactly* the hand they deserve."

FIFTEEN

Ice Cream and Expectations

I slept Friday night without nightmares or interruptions for the first time since I'd left my marital home. When I woke the next morning feeling refreshed, it took me a moment to remember why I felt so weightless, so free. Because I was free. Of Carl's threats, of his power over me and Josie—all of it. I could breathe again, and I wasn't wasting another second of my life thinking about that man.

Josie and I had an extra-special sprinkle, chocolate chip, *and* whipped cream pancake breakfast to celebrate. I didn't put it that way to her, but in my heart it was a celebration. When I'd explained the afternoon before that her daddy's and my divorce was final, she'd been stoic about the whole thing. For as young as she was, she was more aware of what was going on than I'd expected. She hadn't cried, just hugged me, and gone back to playing in Celia's front room.

When the phone rang and it was Jensen, a smile as wide as the Mississippi took over my face.

"Good morning."

"Good morning, beautiful. I was calling to see if you and Miss Josie had plans this afternoon?"

"Not at the moment. Did you have something in mind?"

"I sure do. How does celebratory ice cream sound? I was thinking the three of us could drive on over to Pooler and visit the creamery. They've got all the good stuff."

"That sounds fun. Hang on."

"Hey Josie," I called her in from the porch. "Would you like to go have ice cream with me and Mr. Jensen this afternoon?" I waggled my eyebrows at her, feeling silly.

She was swinging a well-loved Barbie by the arm, her two shoes not matching and her sunglasses askew. "Do they have sprinkles?"

"Oh, Mr. Jensen says it's fancy. I am sure they do. Probably other toppings too, like—"

"Caramel syrup?! Yes, I want to go. We want to go, Mr. Jensen!" She hollered the last line towards the phone, and his answering chuckle let me know he heard her.

I gave her a thumbs up and she wandered back outside with her Barbie doll to play on the swing.

"I'll pick you up at three?"

"Sounds perfect."

"It's a date, Magnolia." I leaned back against the kitchen doorway, as I absorbed the words. It could be a date, now. I blew out a breath and shook off my stupor to go and clean up the breakfast dishes.

I went through the motions with a smile on my face, and heat pooled in my belly at his words long after we'd hung up the phone.

It's *a date*.

I primped and curled significantly more than usual for a visit to an ice cream shop. Granted, *usual* was *not at all*, but still. I thought I looked nice in my cut-off shorts and pretty floral top, freshly done curls and flip-flops. It was the perfect ice cream outfit.

When I heard Jensen's truck pull into the driveway, my stomach went wild with anticipation. *It's a date, it's a date, it's a date* ran through my head on repeat, just like it had all morning. Did that mean we were dating now? Would he ask, or did he just assume? Would he expect *me* to take the lead and make the distinction, since I'd been so insistent we were just friends? Too many questions, no answers to be found.

"Josie! Time to put your shoes on, baby girl!"

She flounced out of her room in a sundress, the beloved Barbie now also in a dress, matching heels, and flower-power sunglasses. I didn't recognize those from her stash, so they must have come from a hidden recess of one of Celia's closets.

Jensen's polite knock at the door made Josie squeal and run that way. I resisted the urge to follow suit, deciding it wouldn't be dignified for someone over the age of six. She flung the door wide and was already talking ninety-to-nothing by the time I made it out onto the porch with them.

"—and I like raspberry ripple. Oh! And chocolate fudge sauce. The hot kind, you know? I think hot chocolate fudge would go really well with raspberry ripple. Oh! What if they have marshmallows! Do you think they have marshmallows?"

Jensen squatted down to her level and answered her with a very serious expression. "Miss Josie, I have it on good authority that not only do they have marshmallows, but they also have sprinkles, chocolate chips, butterscotch chips, chopped up Reese's, caramel chunks, and thirty-three other solid toppings."

Her eyes widened with glee.

"That's mighty specific," I mused, raising an eyebrow suspiciously.

"When one is entertaining beautiful ladies, one must call ahead to make sure they'll be fully satisfied with the offerings." He straightened and gave me a warm smile, before tracing my outfit selections. "You look magnificent, as always."

I snorted. "Last time you saw me, I was wearing my funeral dress and my doctor's appointment flats."

"You wore your funeral dress to court?"

"It was sufficiently morose, either way," I said with a shrug

He shook his head at me but wasn't dissuaded. "Well, you're the best-looking morose woman I've ever seen. Y'all ready to go?"

I looked down, and saw that Josie was still barefoot. "Almost. Shoes, Josie?"

She sighed. "Okay, but I don't see why we can go barefoot in the yard and at our new house, but not in an ice cream parlor. We could eat outside!" She trotted back inside, on the hunt for shoes.

Jensen laughed at her sass. "She is something else."

"Something wild, you mean. Lately, she's been all about the yard and outside. It's nice to see her with some color in her cheeks, but I wish she'd go back to wearing shoes."

He stepped closer, looping an arm around my back lightly and staring into my eyes. "I'm sure, but she's a country girl now. They like to feel the ground under their toes."

I shook my head at the idea that my daughter had lost all her city ways so quickly, but couldn't look away from his magnetic stare.

"So—" I started to ask the million-dollar question, but Josie blew past us, headed straight for Jensen's truck. Startled, I pulled back and watched as she bolted across the yard, neon pink Crocs clutched in her free hand.

"You're supposed to put them on, Jo-jo!" I hollered.

"I will when we get there, Mom!"

Jensen wrapped his hand around mine and tugged me gently down the porch steps. "We better get going, or she'll drive herself there and leave us behind."

"Probably," I muttered my agreement. "Best get a move on, or we'll need second jobs to pay the bill. She's got a real sweet tooth," I joked.

"Me too. Mine seems honed in on a sweet lady, at the moment." I felt the wink he cast over his shoulder to the tips of my hair as he jogged to open the truck door for me.

True to her word, Josie donned her Crocs—over dusty feet—as Jensen parked his truck in front of the quaint ice cream parlor. The sign out front was hand-painted "Peachy Keen Ice Cream" in a swirling font, with a sun-faded peach logo. Inside smelled of fresh waffle cones, with that tantalizing hint of burnt sugar.

Josie darted right up to the display case, and was already pointing out the many, many toppings she wanted before we even made it all the way through the door. The cheerful proprietor behind the case grinned and grabbed a large cup for her.

She and Jensen had several intense discussions about flavor combinations, ice cream overload, and the proper topping-to-base ratios before they had their orders settled. Mine was simple; a waffle cone with two scoops of butter pecan. Jensen insisted on paying, lending credence to my it's-a-real-date theory.

As we clustered around one of the little round tables lining the walls, Josie swung her feet and chattered between bites of her towering ice cream concoction. Suddenly, she froze.

"Mom, I need to go to the bathroom!"

"Okay, let's go." I passed Jensen my cone, which he pretended to take a huge bite of, eliciting a smack on the arm before we walked away.

I leaned against the sink while she was in the stall, quiet for the first time since Jensen had arrived. After I heard the flush, her precious little voice came floating through the door crack.

"Hey, Mom?"

"Yes?"

"Is Mr. Jensen going to be my new dad now?"

"What?" I spluttered, shocked that she'd jumped straight to that conclusion. He'd been around a lot, but we'd been careful that was not a whiff of romance in front of her. "What makes you think that?"

She let herself out of the stall and busied herself washing her hands in the sink before saying anything else. Her eyes were serious, wise beyond her years, when she looked up at me. "He's really nice,

Mom. You smile a lot when he's around, and you didn't with Daddy."

Tears nearly choked me, when I realized how much she'd noticed about my unhappy marriage. God, what a poor example I'd set for her, coasting along unhappily with Carl. Determined not to lay my pain on her shoulders, I forced a smile.

"I don't know, sweetie. But he is really fun, isn't he? Plus, you and he both like the same kind of ice cream."

"Oh yeah, he likes the cool stuff. Not boring nuts like yours." She made a sour face, and tugged the door open to get back to her *cool stuff*, serious conversation instantly forgotten.

I, however, struggled to feign lightness the rest of the trip. Was I moving too quickly, even as careful as I'd been, if Josie thought Jensen was going to be her new daddy? The thoughts weighed heavily on my heart, and the sour taste of doubt dampened my butter pecan bliss.

That night I found myself lying in bed, wrestling with confusion and, if I looked too closely, sadness. Not the emotions I'd expected after a fun and wholesome family date, but there I was. Josie's words had spooked me, and worry had edged its way in that I wasn't taking the time I should to really be alone, focus on Josie, and piece our lives back together. I was operating in reactive mode, and as much as I had developed strong feelings for Jensen already, was that the most important thing?

Almost as if he'd heard me thinking about him, my phone buzzed with a message.

Jensen: You awake?

Maggie: Yes. Everything okay?

The phone rang in my hand, startling me for a second before I answered it.

"Hello, Magnolia," he said, his voice rougher than usual, ruffling my nerves and waking up pesky butterflies I didn't want to feel at the moment.

"Hi, Jensen," I half-whispered, not that Josie could hear me. She'd been snoring softly in her bed, curled up with her squishy frog pillow when I checked on her before my shower.

"I got the feeling something was off this afternoon, when we came home from the ice cream shop. I didn't want to go to bed until I spoke to you and made sure everything was okay." He paused briefly. "That *we* were okay."

I sighed, unsure how to answer. He was too perceptive.

"Did I do something to offend you?" His voice was steady, ever calm amidst my tumultuousness.

"No, not at all. The opposite." I ran a hand through my hair and decided to just be honest with him. "In the bathroom, Josie asked if you were going to be her new daddy. It took me off guard, and just . . ."

"Wow, really?"

"Yeah. She likes you a lot. Does that bother you?" I held my breath, his answer suddenly the most important factor of this conversation.

"Of course not. I'm flattered. I like her too. She's smart, and spunky, and hilarious. It's a rare combo."

I chuckled at that. "You're not wrong, she's something special."

"Just like her mama."

Even over the phone, his words made me blush. "Stop it."

He tsked teasingly at me. "You can't stop the truth, Magnolia."

"Uh-huh." I layered my tone with as much sarcasm as I could fit into two sort-of words. Turns out, that was a lot.

He chuckled at my sass. "Well, if you're sure we're okay, I'd like to invite you on a more grown-up date, say Friday night? I've got something fun in mind, but I don't think it would be appropriate for Josie."

"A grown-up date. Does that mean—" I swallowed, trying to muster my courage. "Does that mean we're dating now? Officially?" I stammered the last bit, in case the first fumblings were unclear.

"Well, it means I'd like us to be. If you'll have me."

"Oh." I was surprised by the answer, even though I'd suspected.

"Are you disappointed?"

"No, of course not. Just surprised, I guess."

"Well then I'll have to make my intentions clearer, so there aren't any more surprises. Can I pick you up on Friday at six?"

"Sure, sounds good. What should I wear?"

"Dress comfy. Good night, Magnolia. Sweet dreams."

"Sweet dreams, Jensen."

Sixteen

Six days. The man had invited me on a date that was six whole days away. That was far too much time for me to analyze what was going on between us, how soon it was, how Josie was affected, and completely second guess my decision to accept.

I'd been lying awake, sleepless with conflict when he called, and I'd *still* accepted. What kind of pull did the man have, that I'd do that? Maybe he'd been to Hogwarts, bought a love potion, and slipped it into my drink the first time I had lunch with him? Ha. I'd *love* to blame my intense attraction on something like that, but I was afraid it was all me.

Over the course of the week, I talked myself into it and out of it roughly a thousand times, and when

Friday morning rolled around, I was still undecided. I'd arrived early for my morning shift at the restaurant, and already had my apron on and was doing some under-table vacuuming when Janie finished her prep and came out onto the floor.

She stood, hand on hip as she watched me aggressively attacking crumbs, my motions jerky and frustrated.

"Why don't you set that down, and have a cup of coffee with me before we open?" she half-yelled, so I could hear her over the vacuum.

I stubbornly persisted for a moment, before giving up and switching off the vacuum. I couldn't ignore Janie. She poured two cups and doctored them up with cream and sugar while I wrapped up the vacuum cord and tucked it away.

She waved me over to a corner booth, and I slid in wordlessly. She passed me one of the cups, and I took a long sip.

"Start talking, honey. You should be much happier for someone who's just left behind a nasty divorce and walked away with everything she wanted. Instead, you're in here harassing the carpet. What's wrong?"

"I wasn't harassing it, I was vacuuming," I insisted.

"Uh-huh. Night shift does that after close. You were working off steam. Let's hear it."

I dropped my head into my hands with a sigh. "It's about Jensen."

"I suspected as much. Usually takes a man like that to make a smart woman like you get off-kilter. What'd he do?"

"He invited me on a date. A real date, as in, we'd be *dating* now."

She arched one eyebrow, and took a pointed sip of her coffee, waiting for me to continue.

"Okay, well, isn't it too soon for that? And Josie's already got expectations, even though he's been just friendly all this time. And now if we make it official . . . I'll have to tell her. Then she'll really get her hopes up, and the whole town will know, and what if—" I stopped, shutting off the word vomit mid-sentence.

Janie reached across the table and squeezed my hand. "Honey, do you like him?"

"Well, of course I like him. He's perfect."

She chuckled. "It sounds like Josie does too, right?"

I nodded and clutched my coffee mug tighter, a lump rising in my throat. *Is Mr. Jensen going to be my new dad, now?* She definitely liked him.

"Okay then. The rest is details. Take it slow. Get to know each other and have a little fun. No one's saying you've got to race down the aisle—though I know at least a few biddies in this town who'd be thrilled if you did, of course. It's normal to feel mixed up after a divorce. It's normal to feel uncertain. You and Josie are going to be just fine."

"But . . . how do I know it's not wrong?"

Confusion crossed her face. "What do you mean 'wrong?'"

"Well . . . when I married Carl, I thought he was the one. The forever one, my one big love. Looking back now, I'm not sure I ever actually loved him. I was infatuated, sure. I was even flattered that he was interested in me. But now I know better. Infatuation and flattery ran out pretty quick, and here I am. I don't know how to tell if he's wrong, too."

Janie sighed a sad sigh. "Honey, you've grown and matured so much since then. The fact that you can look back and see why it was wrong with Carl—not just at the end, but in the beginning—means you *do* know what was wrong. Do you feel those shallow feelings about Jensen, or is it more?"

"I don't know," I admitted sheepishly.

"You do. You just haven't really examined your feelings. Take some time, get to know the boy. Let yourself think about what you truly feel and see where it goes. Don't settle until you find the one you can't live without, and you'll be just fine." She squeezed my hand one more time, and then stood. "You ready to get this place opened up?"

"Yes, ma'am." I stood and put away the vacuum, but as I went through the motions, my heart was still pondering her words. What *did* I feel for Jensen?

After work I picked Josie up from school, helped with her Spring Extravaganza lines, made her an afternoon snack, and packed a sleepover bag before dropping her off with Celia. They'd planned an evening play date with a school friend and were going to the park. I had no idea where we were going or how late we'd be back, so Celia had offered to let Josie sleep over after.

An hour later I was prepped and primped, debating between my favorite blue jeans with a flowy sleeveless blouse and a summer dress. I decided on the jeans. Better to have full coverage when you didn't know what the activity was. What if he was taking me horseback riding, or some adventure activity? He liked the outdoors, so I wouldn't put it past him.

After my dallying over the decision, I'd barely zipped my pants when I heard his knock on the door. I checked my clock as I jogged past to open the door.

Five fifty-seven—the man was punctual, I had to give him that.

"Hey, Jensen," I said a little breathlessly as I hauled the door open.

"Hey, Magnolia. You look amazing, as usual." He leaned forward and pressed a kiss to my cheek, lingering there with his warm skin flush to mine. When he finally pulled back, my heart was racing for reasons besides my impromptu jog down the hall. "Are you ready to go, or do you need a few minutes? I was early, but I didn't want to sit in the truck when I could just come see you now."

"I just need to grab my purse, one second." I held up a finger and walked to the kitchen to grab it.

After I locked up, he took my hand and walked me to his truck where he held the door for me while I climbed up.

Once we were on the road with our fingers linked over the console, I asked, "Sooo, where are we going tonight?"

"Hmm, well, first up we are having dinner at the Sushi place in town—I reserved us a table next to the waterfall. Then, I'd like to keep part two a surprise, if that's okay with you."

"There's two parts? You've been a busy-plan-ning-bee," I teased.

"Absolutely. Do you really want to know, or are you down with being surprised?"

I mulled it over for a moment. "Surprises are good."

"That's my girl!" he said enthusiastically.

A happy little glow suffused me, even over the tiny praise. It was so *easy* when I was with him. It wasn't until we were apart, and I started thinking too much that things got all twisted up. Tonight, I was determined to relax, and try to get to know him on a deeper level. Enjoy myself a little. I'd surely earned at least that much after my last few months of struggle.

When we walked into the sushi restaurant, the hostess led us straight through the restaurant to the back, where the lighting was dim and focused on a cascading water feature. Our table was tucked behind it, making it into a little bubble of privacy for two.

"This is so cool, Jensen. And very private." I leaned as far back as I could without tipping my chair and could barely see the nearest table. "You'd never even know there was a table back here."

He smiled, pleased that I liked it. "I figured privacy would be a good thing, until we had a little more time to settle into this," he admitted. "I know you're not excited about the town knowing we're dating, and I can only cook so many things without having to call my mom. This seemed like a happy medium." He gestured to the protective curtain of water.

My heart squeezed at his thoughtfulness, but also at the idea that he thought I didn't want to be seen with him. Had I given him that impression? "Jensen, I'm not *not* excited about people knowing we're dating. I have no problem being seen with you. I just . . . The gossip makes me uncomfortable. Everyone knows why I moved back to town, and it's embarrassing to think they're all talking about my jacked-up love life. It's not you—you know that, right?"

"Well, I'm glad to hear that. But Magnolia, everybody in this town loves you. They talk, sure. It's a small town, and that's never going to change. But if you think people won't be happy for you, you're wrong. You're already a fan-favorite at Jude's, and nobody would dare say a negative word about Celia's niece. Mostly people are offended on your behalf at how stupid your ex was."

Surprise shot through me at his words. "And you know all this, how?"

"My mom's the only realtor in town, remember? She hears everything. Normally I ignore it, but in this case I asked, since I knew you were uncomfortable, and I wanted to know if there was anything negative you should know about. There wasn't. Half the old men in town are jealous that you'll be off the market, though. Apparently you give them extra sugars for their coffee, and they're all smitten." He snorted.

I was floored. He hadn't just asked her to make fried chicken for me and given me his perfect house to rent. "That's . . . Wow." I didn't know what to say.

"Too much? I'm sorry. Maybe I should let Merle challenge me to that duel for your affections, after all."

I couldn't help it, I laughed hard at that image. He was an octogenarian who came into the diner every morning for coffee and to read his newspaper. We'd had some long chats about his time in the war and his late wife, Belinda.

"Merle is a sweetheart, but I'll stick with you, thanks."

"Does that mean you're okay with a regular restaurant table next time?" His lips quirked up at one corner, but I could see the hopefulness shadowed in his eyes.

"Goodness, I've been absolutely awful to you. You've been amazing every step along the way, and I've got you thinking I'm embarrassed to be seen with you. It's a miracle you're even interested in a next time." I let my hands fall in my lap and worried the hem of my shirt with one hand.

"Hey, now, don't talk like that." He stuck a hand out palm up for me to hold, and I reluctantly settled my fingers into his. He traced small trails against my palm, and a shiver ran through me at the contact. "I'm not mad, Magnolia. I understand. I'm just not sure how to help you with it, other than respect your wishes. When you're comfortable being more open, we'll be more open. We don't have to take out a billboard announcing anything."

"Is there even a billboard in town?" I teased, trying to lighten the mood.

"All right, Ms. Smarty-pants. No, there isn't a bill-board in town."

We both chuckled as the waitress came and took our order. The rest of dinner went more smoothly, chatting and enjoying the delicious Japanese food. He ordered some interesting-looking raw sushi, and I stuck with the nicely cooked hibachi options.

By the time we finished, I was stuffed and incredibly curious about what he had planned for part two of this date.

Once we were back in his truck and headed out of town, curiosity got the better of me. "So, do I get to know where we're going now?"

"No ma'am, sorry."

"But it's part two! Part one ended."

My bargaining did nothing to sway him. We drove a good forty-five minutes before a bright light ahead caught my attention.

"What is that?"

"Part two," he said smugly as a huge projector screen and a hillside full of couples setting out blankets came into view.

"Oh, an outdoor movie! That's amazing!" I looked over at him with excitement, and he flashed me a happy smile before parking in the lot.

He climbed out and grabbed a couple of large blankets and a small cooler before coming around to my side. I didn't wait for him to open the door, meeting him at the back tailgate instead.

"Hey, I'm supposed to open the door for you." He frowned at me.

I chuckled. "You usually do. Every once in a while I'll be fine, like now when your hands are full."

"Yeah, but this is our first date, and I'm trying to impress you."

"You've been impressing me for weeks, Jensen." I rolled my eyes at him.

"Really, now? Do tell." There was that cheesy grin that I was coming to love so much.

I whacked him on the arm playfully and followed him across the grass to a nice open spot. We spread out the bigger blanket, and got settled in the middle, our shoulders brushing casually. A moment later, the opening credits for Sleepless in Seattle rolled across the giant screen, and I leaned my head against him with a sigh.

He was solid and warm, and the whole time I watched Meg Ryan and Tom Hanks on the screen, my mind kept coming back to Jensen. All the ways he'd supported me, even when he knew I hadn't wanted to date. Even now that I was a free woman, he was taking his time, and respecting my boundaries. He was handsome and kind, financially stable and had his life together. It was still beyond me why he wanted to tie himself to me, but maybe it was time to stop questioning that, once and for all. Maybe he was just a blessing, and I was too busy worrying to see that.

A short while later I shivered, and he passed me the second blanket. I spread it over my legs and snuggled closer against his side. He wrapped his arm around my shoulders, and we felt so right together. Like two pieces of a puzzle, sliding perfectly into place.

The movie had finally sucked me in, and I lost track of time, cozy as I was. I felt Jensen shift but didn't think anything of it, until his worried whisper dragged me back into the present.

"Magnolia, we've got to go!"

"What's wrong?"

"It's Josie. Celia's been calling, but she wasn't able to get through to you."

I frantically patted around for my phone but realized I didn't have it. "Oh my God, I think I left it in the truck! What's going on? Did she say what was happening?" Panic washed over me in a wave, threatening to pull me under as I grabbed up the blanket and my water bottle, ready to bolt straight back to my baby. What if Carl had shown up? He'd been quiet since the divorce, but I wasn't truly sure if that would hold.

Jensen grabbed my arm, his touch firm and gentle at the same time. "I don't know, Mags, but we'll get loaded up and call her as soon as we're in the truck."

"Okay, we've got to hurry."

By the time I finished speaking, he already had the cooler and blanket, and we were rushing through the last few rows of disgruntled couples to get back to his truck.

I practically ran to the back and threw in the blanket, before snatching the passenger door open and frantically rooting around for my phone. It was in my purse, which I'd tucked under the seat so I wouldn't have to carry it out into the field. I snatched it up and cursed under my breath when I saw several missed calls, a voicemail, and a text from Celia which simply said, "Call me—urgent."

Jensen was in and driving in a flash. "Buckle up, Magnolia, and we'll get you there."

I absently clicked the seatbelt into place as I dialed Celia's number, ignoring the voicemail. It rang four torturous times before it dropped to voicemail. I hung up and dialed again. After the second time it went to voicemail, I finally opened her message.

"Maggie, honey, it's me. I'm so sorry, but we need you to come back from your date. We were at the playground, and Josie was hanging upside down on the monkey bars, when she slipped and fell. We are heading to the hospital for an X-ray, and she's scared and asking for you. Meet us at the children's hospital in Savannah as soon as you can."

I flung a hand out. "Jensen, stop. Head to the children's hospital. They're not in Adele."

He checked both directions and made a wide u-turn, half-slinging me against the door. "What's wrong, did she say?"

"She was hanging upside down on the monkey bars and fell. She didn't say what was wrong, only that Josie's hurt and scared. Oh God, Jensen. I'm the worst mother ever."

"You are not," he insisted, but I ignored him. I sunk my head into my hands, panicked sobs racking me.

I needed to pull it together, but all I could think was that my daughter needed me, and I was too busy on a date to be there for her. I hadn't even thought about my phone.

We rode the hour to the hospital in tense silence, with me on the edge of my seat as worry and horrendous guilt built up like a geyser, waiting to erupt. He pulled up in front of the emergency entrance, and I leapt from the truck before it had fully stopped.

"I'll be in as soon as I find a spot!"

I froze, and turned back to him, my heart as cold as the arctic tundra. The few feet between us felt like an impassable divide. "Jensen, I don't think that's a good idea."

He drew back, shocked. "What? I want to be here for you, for both of you."

"No, I—I can't do this right now. Tonight was great, but I'm a single mom, and I have responsibilities. I can't see you again, I'm so sorry. This can't happen again." The last words came out broken, even my voice rebelling against what was necessary.

"Magnolia, don't say that, please. Going on a date didn't cause—"

I held up a hand, as if it would shield me from his words, and from the knives shredding my heart at having this conversation. "Jensen, I can't right now. I have to go."

"Magnolia, I'm not going to just leave you here. I love you; can't you see that?!" He nearly yelled it he was so desperate to get me to listen.

The words battered me, making me withdraw even further. I couldn't dwell on that—I had to go find my baby.

"Please, go home. I'm so sorry." Like the coward I was, I turned my back on him and darted inside, choking on a sob. My heart was breaking, and I knew in my soul that the look on his face as I abandoned him would haunt me for the rest of my life.

I plunged through the hospital doors, frantic as I told the woman behind the registration desk who I was looking for. She directed me to the right room, where Celia was pacing behind a glass door with a haggard look on her face. I threw myself into her arms, and she hugged me so tightly it felt like my ribs were going to crack.

"Maggie! I'm so glad you got the message. I get no service in this hospital, so I couldn't call you again after we got here."

"Where's Josie?" I surveyed the empty room, the child-sized hospital bed in the middle making my stomach lurch.

"She's getting a scan. X-ray or CT? I can't remember which they said first."

"So, it's serious?" My voice wavered, and I sunk out of her grip and into one of the hard, straight-backed chairs next to the bed.

"We don't know for sure, but the doctor seemed confident she'd be okay. They are being cautious, since she was upside down when she fell."

"Was she awake when they took her back?"

"Oh, yes. Awake and talking up a storm. That child has already wrapped three nurses and a transport fellow around her little finger." She shook her head at the thought, then focused back in on me. "Is Jensen parking the car?"

I hesitated, unsure what to tell her. "No, I sent him home."

Her eyebrows shot up so high, they disappeared behind her bangs. "And he just went? I wouldn't expect that."

"No, he didn't want to go, but I broke up with him. I made him go."

"Oh, honey, no! Why?" She leaned down and hugged me again, but I didn't know what to tell her. Shame, embarrassment, sorrow, and worry were making a soup of my brain.

The glass door sliding open further grabbed our attention, and I bolted back to my feet as they pushed Josie in the door on a stretcher.

"Josie!"

"Mama! You're here!"

I wanted to reach out and snatch her to me for a hug, but the nurse urged me back.

"Please give us a moment, ma'am, we're going to move her back into the bed and then you can see her. *Gently.*"

I bristled, instantly disliking her. I watched with my heart in my throat as they gathered the sheet at each corner, and swiftly swept her from the stretcher into the bed. She looked so tiny, when they lowered the sheet, and unnaturally pale under the fluorescent lights. The nurse fiddled with some monitoring equipment, but I ignored her as I burst forward and hovered over Josie.

Tear tracks marred her beautiful cheeks, and my heart broke all over again.

"I was so scared, Mama. I'm so glad you're here." She reached across herself and clung to my shoulders with her left arm, her right unmoved on the bed.

"I know, baby, I was scared too. But I'm here now and I am not leaving your side, not for a minute. You'll be superglued to me, if I have anything to say about it."

She giggled, the tiny sound like fresh rain on my parched heart. I needed my baby happy and healthy, not lying in this bed hurt and scared. I squeezed her left hand and leaned back to look her over. "What hurts?"

She pointed at her elbow, and the back of her shoulders. "I fell back here, and my elbow hurts so *bad*." Tears sprang into her eyes again just thinking about it, and I shushed her soothingly.

"I know, honey, I'm so sorry. It's going to be okay, though. They're going to fix you right up and get you feeling better."

"We absolutely are, young lady. I have good news!" A male doctor with a booming voice strode in, a jovial smile on his face. "You gave us a scare, but your noggin and your neck are A-okay. Your elbow is going to need a bit of TLC, though."

He popped a few scans into a viewing frame next to the bed and pointed out different spots on the head and neck portions. "We were primarily worried about these areas, given the angle of her fall. However, her movement is excellent, and she shows no sign of concussion. My best guess after seeing the scans is that she twisted on the way down, and the right arm took the brunt of it."

He switched out the scans, showing us a close up of the elbow, and the two bones running down her forearm. "Interestingly enough the radius and ulna are intact, but the capitulum of the humerus has a fracture."

He pointed to a small spot on one of the bones, and I had to squint to try to make out the difference between what looked like a bunch of foggy blurs to me.

"So, because of the position of this and the possibility of chipping if it were re-injured, we're going to be putting a cast on tonight before you can go home. We'll get you a waterproof one, and you can pick any color you like." He lowered his voice, and hunkered down to get closer to her level, gray eyes sparkling with mischief. "They even have glittery cast materials now, so you can get a glitter stripe at the end if you ask nicely."

"Oh, I will. I can be very nice." Josie was mesmerized by his charm, whereas I was just relieved that she hadn't suffered any more serious injuries. "Can Mama come with me?"

"Absolutely! She can help you choose a color." He beamed at her.

She was going to be okay. In a cast, but okay.

SEVENTEEN

Wise Council

THREE WEEKS LATER

For the second time in my life, I found myself rolling a giant bucket of clean silverware into paper napkins, staring at a bunch of overly enthusiastic PTA members. The difference this time was that it wasn't my first day, and I had other tables to tend to, and somewhere to be tonight. Irritation crawled up my spine, despite my best efforts to ignore it and remain pleasant.

Today's talking points felt frivolous, and if they didn't get out of here soon, I was liable to dump a pitcher of Granny's Famous right over one of their heads. Of course, then I'd lose my job, be unable to pay my rent, and be the talk of the town all over again when things had just settled down after the breakup with Jensen.

Despite our discretion with our one real date, everybody knew and everybody talked. Granted, we'd gone from three plus visits every week at the diner to zero overnight, so it wasn't exactly a secret to all and sundry. Frankly, it stung to be back in the same place as I was day one, waiting on the dadgum PTA, knowing that this time Jensen wouldn't be walking through the door to charm me.

I slammed one of the sets of silverware into the tub, and Sue stopped filling a glass to look over at me with concern etched into her face. "You all right, hon? You seem . . . tense today."

I could tell she was mincing words, trying not to tick me off further, and I felt awful. "I'm sorry, Sue. It's the PTA. They're getting to me today."

"Uh-huh. Taking out your life's problems on the silverware bucket can be satisfying, but it rarely solves anything. Why don't you let me finish up with the PTA, and I'll leave your tip for you to pick up tomorrow. You get out of here early, go blow off some steam."

My shoulders sagged with relief at the kind offer, even though it pricked my pride to hear the concern lacing her voice.

"Thank you, Sue. I could kiss you."

"Go on and get, now. You need the time." She shooed me to the back, where I ditched my apron, grabbed my keys, and clocked out. Janie wasn't in, but Sue would tell her for me when she came back.

When life got you down, there was one place guaranteed to pick you up like no other. When I pushed the door open and the smells of Celia and Bea's baking washed over me, I could already feel the tension leaking out of my shoulders. I'd get a croissant, and haunt one of the window tables with a book until I felt better.

I hadn't even made it to the glass counter yet when Celia's voice came from the side, not behind the counter or in the kitchen like usual.

"Maggie, honey, I wasn't expecting you today. Don't you have another hour left on your shift?" Celia was blowing on a cup of hot coffee, sitting at the window table across from Janie, a smorgasbord of pastries on a tray in front of them. Janie didn't say a word, despite being my boss and likely having the same exact question.

"Well, yes. But it was slowing down, and Sue offered to finish up the PTA meeting for me so that I could have a little me-time. So, I came in search of croissants and coffee."

"Always a good idea," Janie said with a gracious smile. She was the best manager I'd ever had and was so understanding.

"Come sit with us, I'll get you a cup." Celia pushed back from the table and took her time fixing me a fresh cup of coffee. I chose a cherry-almond croissant from their selection and moaned with the first bite.

"Where's Bea today?" I asked as Celia sat back down and slid a perfect, creamy coffee in front of me.

"Mm, day off for wedding planning. I believe they are scouting venues today, and meeting with a few photographers."

"Oh, that's exciting," Janie gushed.

"Yep, the plans are coming right along." Celia eyed me speculatively. "So, Maggie, what's going on?"

I looked down at my coffee mug and shrugged. "Just having a bad day, I guess."

She snorted. "Now that's bull if ever I heard it."

My head jerked up in surprise.

Janie tsked at her. "Celia, don't pry. You know things have been hard lately."

"Of course I know, but that doesn't mean she doesn't need to talk about it. You can't walk around in a bad mood for the rest of your life, because things went wrong with a man. So, let's hear it. What's *really* going on?"

I blew out a long breath, trying to figure out where to start. I didn't really want to talk about it, because it hurt. But Aunt Celia was right; I had been in a bad mood for weeks. Snapping at customers, short tempered with Josie's antics, and sleeping poorly most nights. Something had to give.

"I screwed things up and I don't know how to move past it."

"Go on, honey," Janie said, and rubbed my shoulder supportively.

So I did. I laid it all out there; Jensen's support, his patience and kindness, then Josie's attachment to him forming so quickly. My reluctance to commit to someone so soon after things ended with Carl, and how I didn't trust my own decisions. Then, the fateful night. Even telling them how I'd ended things so abruptly hurt, my throat tightening almost impassably as the last words slipped out.

I remembered every single detail from the damp concrete crunching under my feet to the pain lines etched between his eyebrows as he frowned from the driver's seat of the truck. The memory of him had been tattooed on my heart, a lingering wound that wouldn't stop aching, even weeks later.

Janie's sadness was palpable on one side, but Celia had a different air about her. Consideration. She tapped her fingers on the table while she watched me, debating what to say.

"What do you think now? Do you think ending it was the right decision?"

"I still don't know. It hurts, but Josie has to be my number one priority, no matter what."

"That's noble of you dear, but misguided."

Her frank words surprised me yet again.

"Honey, when you were married to Carl, you had more to take care of than Josie alone. When you lived with me, you had more to take care of than Josie. And now, even by yourself with her, you still have a household to run, a job to work, and other commitments to her school, the community, and your extended family. You can't put yourself and Josie on an island, as if there isn't enough of you to go around."

A sob rattled in my chest, trying to break free. The choked sniffle that escaped was undignified, and I was embarrassed as another, and another followed.

"That's it, sweetie. Let it out. It's okay to feel hurt—now we just have to figure out what to do about it." Celia rubbed my shoulders soothingly, and after a while, I regained my composure.

"I'm sorry, I just . . . I feel like I'm stretched too thin already. I want so bad to be everything for Josie, make up for what she's lost. Then I let myself get distracted by the first man that pays me a bit of attention, and I wasn't there when she needed me. She got hurt, Celia! Really hurt. And I was on a date."

I dropped my head to my forearms, wallowing in my shortcomings. I had let everyone down.

"Well, are you angry with me?" Celia asked.

I lurched upright, horrified. "What? No! Of course not. Why would I be angry with you?"

"Well, if you can blame yourself—and Jensen, by extension—for Josie getting hurt, surely you blame me. I was the one watching her when she fell. Should I have been standing right under her the whole time she played on the playground?"

I shook my head. "Aunt Celia, even if you wanted to, you couldn't keep up with her the whole time. She moves so fast, you would be running like crazy and she'd still get past you. She's usually fine. Accidents happen."

"So, what would you have done if you'd been there, and not with Jensen?"

"Well, I . . ." I looked down at my half-drunk coffee, realization setting in. "I couldn't have done anything differently. I'd have scooped her up and run her to the hospital, just like you did."

Janie placed a hand gently over mine, and I looked over at her. "Honey, motherhood is hard. Divorce is hard. Dating is hard. Heck, balancing daily life is hard. You are never going to be perfect at it, but that doesn't mean you aren't doing just fine. Because you are doing the best you can, and that *is* enough."

Celia cut in, "You're allowed to have a life of your own, in addition to taking care of your sweet girl. If you keep cutting yourself off, you're going to get burnt out, and that's no good for her. She needs to see you happy and thriving, living a good life. That's all she needs. You, loving her and living a good life."

"How did you two get so wise?" I sniffled, wanting to cry at the unconditional support, but feeling like I'd done far too much of that already. No, I was done crying. Hopefully.

"We're getting old. Comes with the territory," Celia said sarcastically. "Now, let's talk about Jensen. Do you still have feelings for him, or do you think it was the right decision to break it off?"

"I miss him every day. I don't think I'll ever forget that look of betrayal on his face when I walked away."

"Why don't you tell him that?" Janie suggested. "He's a good boy, I'm sure he'd given you a second chance."

"I can't do that, Janie. I took all the good he poured into me, and I threw it in his face. He deserves to be done with me, to move on. I was awful to him, and I don't deserve another shot." I grimaced, the truth in those words testing my resolve not to cry already. But I held strong.

"Well, don't give up hope. You never know when a chance to make things right will present itself."

"Maybe," I said, unconvinced.

"Just promise me that if you do get the opportunity, you will trust your gut. And give him the chance to surprise you."

There was no way he'd be willing to risk his heart on me a second time. He told me he loved me, and I walked away.

I couldn't see any way to come back from that, no matter how much I wished otherwise.

Eighteen

Spring Extravaganza

Another week flew by, and after my talk with Aunt Celia and Janie, I was feeling better day by day. I was even considering the possibility of talking to Jensen, at least to apologize, if an opportunity presented itself. Tonight, however, my focus was solely on Josie.

The day for the Spring Extravaganza at school had arrived, and she was beyond excited. Her pink flower costume matched her cast perfectly, the glitter stripe adding real flair to her spins, which she'd been practicing all week—to the detriment of my one and only flower vase.

A shattered vase was small potatoes, though, compared to her excitement. It filled the house—her joy was contagious. And tonight was the night. We drove through town to the elementary school, and the gym parking lot was already over half-filled. By the time the curtain rose, I imagined, it would be a full house.

I parked the car and opened my door to get out, but Josie sat frozen in the back seat, her pink flower costume splayed around her. Popping open her door, I crouched down so I could get on eye level with her.

"What's wrong, baby girl?"

She turned to me with panic in her eyes. "Mom, what if I forget all my steps? The flower petal dance is the best part of the whole play!" Tears brimmed on her lower lids, and I leaned in to unbuckle her and wrap her in a bear hug.

"Baby, you are going to do great. We'll practice backstage again, but I've seen you do it a hundred times this week at home. You know it, you're just feeling nervous. And that's okay."

"Are you sure?"

"Absolutely. Come on, we've got time for another practice run once we get you backstage." I held out my hand in offering, and she took it.

As it turned out, we had time for three practice runs before the teacher called for all the kids to line up, and the parents to take their seats. I gave her one last peck on the cheek and darted out and up the aisle to the third row where Celia had saved my seat. We were smack in the center, so I should get a pretty good video of my beautiful pink flower doing her petal dance.

"How's our girl?" Celia asked in a hushed tone once I was settled.

"Good, she was nervous, but she knows it backwards and forwards. She'll be twenty-five and doing the petal dance on some social media site."

Celia snorted, but didn't argue. Weird things were trendy, after all. "Did you see who was here on your way up?"

"Everybody, I imagine." I glanced around the theater as the lights dimmed, and as I'd suspected it was a packed-out house. "Oh look, there's Janie and Beau." I waved off to the left, and they waved back. Their grandson was in the grade above Josie.

"No, that's not who I meant. Back row, towards the right aisle." She gestured discreetly over her shoulder without turning around.

Curious, I half turned in my seat and scanned the back row. There were quite a few sullen teenage siblings, playing on their phones, a few latecomer parents and then . . . my breath whooshed out of my chest at the sight of him.

Jensen.

Sitting on the back row, tension clear in his shoulders even underneath the park ranger's uniform that he looked devastatingly handsome in. The dim lighting did nothing to diminish his good looks, and my stomach gave an anxious flip-flop just thinking about why he was here. It had been so long ago that Josie had invited him, surely that wasn't why?

He glanced around the gymnasium-turned-auditorium, and I quickly faced back forward, lest I get caught staring.

I didn't say a word back to Celia, just stared straight ahead and sat stiff as a board as the curtain rose, my mind on a million things besides the dancing lines of bumble bees filling the stage, sequined costumes sparkling under the spotlights.

The ninety-minute program passed with painstaking slowness. Josie's petal dance went perfectly, her swirls and twirls the best I'd seen of all her practices. Celia and I cheered at the top of our lungs when they'd sashayed off the stage after. But the rest of the time, I spent obsessing over whether or not I could feel Jensen's eyes drilling into the back of my skull.

Was he glaring? Was he longing? Maybe worst of all, was he indifferent? Ninety minutes was plenty of time for me to imagine all the possible scenarios, none of them good.

When the final song ended and all the kids came out and assembled for the final bows, the room shook with the strength of everyone's applause. As they filed off to the sides, grins stretched wide, the lights came up in the gym, and people streamed into the aisle to meet their children.

Josie's class was meant to meet at a specific spot outside the gym, so Celia and I headed that way. As we made our slow progress down the crowded aisle, I couldn't help my gaze traveling to Jensen, where he stood like a handsome Greek statue against the back wall. Our eyes connected, and a frisson of heat flowed through my veins. It had been a solid month, and I reacted like he'd been kissing me and telling me he loved me just yesterday, and I hadn't screwed everything up.

I kept my eyes locked on him, as each mincing step brought us closer. Despite the connection I still felt so strongly, I couldn't read his expression. He kept his face carefully neutral, pleasant but not terribly interested in the hubbub on every side.

The closer Celia and I got to him, the more anxiety bubbled up. He wasn't responding, he wasn't leaning into me. He wasn't even smiling, not a true smile. The polite smile on his face was weak, lacking the usual life and energy he had in everything he did. My goofy, sweet Jensen.

Finally, we drew abreast of his row. Celia waved for him to join us, and he stepped into the aisle next to her.

Not me.

The fissure in my heart caused by our breakup yawned wider, threatening to engulf me, but if he could keep things civil, I could too. I breathed out through my nose, determined not to let my sadness show. I didn't get to be the sad one, when I'd broken things between us. He wasn't here for me; he was here for Josie. That was painfully clear, as I stared at his broad shoulders ahead of me.

Celia led us to the proper spot, where flower petal-clad girls and bumblebee boys swarmed excitedly to their families. Josie spotted us and bolted, tackling me around the waist in a crushing hug. When she pulled back to chatter excitedly to Celia and spotted Jensen, she lost it.

"Mr. Jensen! You came, you came!"

"I sure did, sweet girl. I wouldn't dream of missing your big show. I brought you a little something to say congratulations, too." He held up a single, long-stemmed pink rose, wrapped in pink tissue and tied with a big bow.

She nearly swooned into the floor. "You brought me a flower?! It's soooo pretty. Mama, look! It's so pretty. Mr. Jensen picks the best flowers, doesn't he?" She held it out for me to admire.

A stone of regret lodged itself in my chest, as I remembered a beautiful bouquet he'd brought me. Struggling to keep the emotion out of my voice, I answered her, "Absolutely, baby. It's lovely, just like you. You did so well tonight! Your pirouette was perfection." I kissed my fingers dramatically, and she giggled, clutching the precious bloom to her chest.

"I'm starving. Who's ready for pizza to celebrate?" Celia asked, eliciting a feminine squeal from Josie.

"I am! Can we invite Sherise's family? They're right there!" She pointed to a family a few steps away, and Celia nodded.

"Absolutely! Come on, we'll go ask." She shot me a pointed look over her shoulder as she ushered Josie away.

Jensen and I stood there awkwardly, his hands in his pockets, mine clenched together in front of me. It was the only awkward moment he and I had ever truly shared, and I tried my best to work through it.

"Thank you for coming this evening. It means a lot to Josie, as you can see. I . . . I wasn't expecting you, after everything." My words trailed off to a murmur at the end.

He grimaced, the first hint of pain he'd allowed to break through since I'd noticed him. "I couldn't not show up for Josie."

God, if only Carl had felt one tenth of the conviction in his tone, I wouldn't have had the past six months of misery I'd been through.

"I know, and I appreciate it more than you'll ever know." My voice cracked, and I hurried to clear my throat to cover it.

His eyes searched mine, really looking at me for the first time. "How have you been?"

What to say? The truth, that I'd been awful? Or a polite gloss over? "It's been hard." I couldn't answer his sincerity with anything less than honesty. He didn't deserve a glib response.

"Yeah, it has." He looked down at the floor and scuffed his work boot on the concrete absently.

We stood there in silence until Josie barrelled back in, beaming like the sun on a cloudless day. "Mr. Jensen, are you coming to the pizza place with us? Sherise's family is going to come, too!"

He dropped down to a crouch, beaming right back at her. "Not tonight, sweetheart. You have a good dinner with your friends, and we'll try another time."

She got a sly look on her face and leaned in to whisper in his ear.

He chuckled and nodded. "Absolutely." He ruffled her hair and stood to leave. "Celia." He gave her a warm smile and a nod, and paused before turning to me, "Magnolia."

The sound of my name on his lips was devastating in its perfection. It was everything, and it was good-bye.

"I'll see you both around." With a final wave to Josie, he left.

Celia and Josie had bounded off to her car for the ride to the pizza place, leaving me to ride the few minutes alone. I didn't mind the reprieve; seeing Jensen had rocked me to the core. He was such a good man, and I'd treated him terribly.

My eyes were locked on the pavement, and I was engaged in a serious round of self-loathing and re-gret when a voice from the side froze me in place.

"Maggie, darling." Carl stood there, leaning against the bumper of my car in one of his work suits, a vicious sneer on his face.

To think I'd ever found him handsome.

"What do you want, Carl?" I tried not to sound as weary as I felt, but the man was like the bad news that wouldn't quit.

"Oh, just to applaud you on your shark of a lawyer's courtroom tricks. I didn't think you had it in you." He looked me up and down, clearly in disapproval of my comfortable jeans and ponytail. Carl had hated it when I didn't look perfect, and I was happier the minute I'd left him—and his antiquated expectations—behind.

"He wasn't a shark. He just pointed out all the crap *you* tried to pull on me." I propped a hand on my hip, starting to get riled up.

He scoffed. "Drop the act, Magnolia. You're no longer the sweet girl I married. What happened to you? When did you get so bitter?"

My jaw dropped at his audacity, and his blindness. He had to ask? I'd fallen for him when I was too young to know better, and he'd been the one to throw a cold glass of reality in my face. In my naivete I hadn't realized that Carl's ambition made him cold, and our marriage had lacked anything resembling the warmth that radiated from Jensen like a crackling fire. Carl was all cold calculation, and I was too young and lovestruck to see it. Not anymore.

"Listen, Carl, you can spew whatever hatefulness you want, but it doesn't change a dang thing. We're done, and that's that. You don't have to like me any more, and I certainly don't like you. Why did you even come all this way? It wasn't to see Josie's play." I gestured to the packed parking lot, streaming with families leaving the show.

He cast his eyes briefly over at the school gymnasium, but didn't mention our daughter. Jerk. "I came to deliver your *check*, of course. Today is the deadline." He pulled a small envelope from his suit pocket, and held it out like he'd done me some sort of favor by following the court order.

His showing up here like this, trying to take me down a peg after everything just proved once again that women were nothing more than props to him. Luckily, I was done being his plaything.

I took the check, and shoved it into my back pocket without looking at it. "You have a nice life, Carl. Don't come here again." I turned my back on him, heading straight for the front seat. He could get off the bumper, or fall over when the car moved out from under him. I didn't care which.

"Bitterness doesn't suit you, Magnolia. I'm sure your new boy-toy will figure that out and get tired of it soon enough."

I spun on my heel, and stepped into his personal space. I glared up at him. "Careful, Carl, your miserable personality is showing. Wouldn't want your model friend to hear you were broke *and* mean now, would we?"

He narrowed his eyes, returning my glare. To my surprise, after a long moment of standing toe to toe, he was the one to back down. "Good riddance, Maggie. Don't come crawling back when you realize your new man-candy is a step down." He shoved his hands into his pockets, and stalked across the parking lot.

It was unpleasant, sure. But deep down, all I felt was satisfaction. He'd tried to hurt and belittle me, yet he was the one who'd tucked tail and run. He didn't have the power to hurt me any more.

Nineteen

Dancing in the Moonlight

That night, Josie fell into bed like a felled tree. She was lightly snoring when I clicked the door shut, and I breathed a sigh of relief. It had been a great day, but a *long* day. As I took my shower and dried my hair, I couldn't stop replaying every interaction with Jensen from the evening. From when my eyes landed on his perfect face to the way he'd said my name before he left—it was everything and not nearly enough.

I climbed into bed with a groan, my shoulders stiff from sitting in the too-small chairs for the play. I tossed, I turned, and I couldn't get Jensen out of my head. I'd been half convinced I'd never see him again, after he'd stopped visiting Jude's cold turkey. For him to show up tonight, though, made me question everything.

He was such a good man; he had been from the start. He'd accepted my every flaw, and not once had he judged me for the trainwreck of my life. And I'd just dumped him, cold and flat. It was wrong. It was so *wrong*.

I sat up and checked the clock. It was still fairly early, and I was betting Celia was awake. Excitement thrummed in my belly at the idea that had just come to me. Was it too crazy, though?

Pushing through the hesitation, I grabbed my phone and made a call. "Can you come over? I need to run out for a while. I'll owe you, big time."

By the time I hung up, I was already out of bed, and slipping out of my pajamas and into a pair of jeans and a long t-shirt.

Not fifteen minutes later, Celia's compact SUV pulled up to the house. I was waiting for her on the porch, keys and purse clutched in hand.

She looked me up and down before giving me a quick nod of approval. "Are you heading where I think you are?"

I nodded, nervous butterflies filling me.

"Good, it's about time." She marched up the stairs and went inside without a backwards glance. I bolted to the car and hummed tunelessly as I crossed the dark streets. When I pulled up in front of the cute blue house, disappointment rocked through me. There was nothing but a small black sedan out front.

Regardless, I made myself go up and knock.

"Hi, is Jensen home?" I asked a young guy in jeans and a sports jersey.

"Nah, he went to see some chick, and didn't even wait for the game to end. He'll probably be back in an hour or two. Want to leave a message?" He looked longingly back over his shoulder, where I could hear a sports announcer yelling excitedly.

"No, no thank you." I took a step back, and he closed the door.

Some chick.

I'd waited too long, and he'd already moved on. No wonder he'd come to the play. I was no danger to him now that he'd found someone new. He could honor his word to a little girl, and not have to worry about her shrew of a mother.

No. I tamped the bitterness down. He was right to move on, even though it felt like my heart was being crushed to dust under a millstone. I'd left him. I'd thrown his affections away like they meant nothing, when really they'd been everything; my unwavering lighthouse in the storms of life.

As I drove home, my heart was heavy. It wasn't what I'd hoped for, but at least now I knew. It had to be enough, even if it was the worst mistake I'd made in a long line of questionable decisions.

When I pulled into the familiar driveway, my heart nearly stopped dead in my chest. There in my driveway was an oversized white park ranger's truck. The porch light was on, glowing cheerily down on him where he sat perched on the front steps.

I turned off the car with numb fingers and climbed out, staring with disbelief. He was here. He'd come *here.*

My feet carried me right to him, as if pulled by his magnetism. When I stopped, all I could do was stare into those soulful green eyes, mesmerized by his very presence.

"You're here."

"I am. You weren't, though . . ."

"I went to see you. Your roommate? Friend? Someone told me you'd left." I ran an agitated hand through my curls at the memory.

"Friend; Joe. I live alone. He came over to watch the football game, and I bailed. I told him he could stay and finish the game," he explained.

"Ahh."

"Yeah, I just kept thinking about a certain gorgeous woman and couldn't focus on football."

The silence drew between us, taut as a bowstring. I wanted so badly to lean into him, pour out all my woes and beg him to take me back. He might say no, of course . . . but he was *here*—that meant something.

"I owe you so many apologies," I said. "You were everything kind and good to me and Josie, and I was so scared, I pushed you away." Regret tried to choke me, but I pushed through. "I know I don't deserve your forgiveness, but I wanted you to know that I regret how that night ended. I wish I could go back, and . . ." I stopped, feeling the ramble coming on. "I'm so sorry, Jensen."

"I'm sorry, too." He stood, and reached forward to hold my elbows, cupping me lightly as if I were a butterfly he didn't want to crush. "I shouldn't have given up so easily. I knew you were scared; I knew Josie was hurt, and I should have insisted—come with you anyways, been there for you." He stopped, and the pain in his eyes was deep when he spoke again. "But I thought I was intruding where I wasn't welcome, and, frankly, it hurt. So, I called myself giving you space, and retreated."

"I don't blame you; I was in a bad state of mind that night." I shook my head, the memory of Josie in that hospital bed still haunting me.

"I know, Magnolia. I do." He reached up and threaded strong fingers into my curls, sending a wild shiver through me. His touch was electric, lighting up all my nerves and making me sway towards him.

"Can you ever forgive me?" I asked.

"I already have," he whispered, leaning close to my ear. "I already have."

I closed my eyes, as relief washed over me. A single tear escaped and rolled down my cheek. I reached up to dash it away, but he beat me to it. His thumb swept gently over my cheek, trapping the tear and smoothing it away.

He kept stroking me, soothing and warming and riling me up, with the most innocent of touches. I leaned into it, the warmth of him filling up all the tiny cracks my heart had splintered into.

"Can you forgive me for not being there?" His tone was low, and the uncertainty in it gave me pause. He'd come back, not knowing whether he'd be rejected again.

"There's nothing to forgive, Jensen. I've regretted those words from the instant they came out of my mouth. But I was too scared to see another way."

"And now?" he asked, his thumb pausing its languid trail across my cheek as he leaned back to take in my expression.

I sighed and looked up at him. "Now, I'm hoping you'll give me another chance. I love you too, Jensen. Against all common sense, despite the fear and all that's happened in the past few months . . . I love you. More than I've loved anyone but Josie, ever."

He smiled, the grin spreading slowly across his face like a sunrise until his entire face was lit with irrepressible joy.

"Those are the prettiest words I've ever heard, Magnolia Abbott. From the prettiest lips." His thumb moved again, this time brushing my bottom lip and making me shudder with desire.

He leaned in and captured my lips with his, and his kiss was like coming home. He was warm, and strong, and right. Everything I had ever wanted, but never thought I'd be able to have. I leaned into his warm chest, my fingers twining into his shirt possessively. I never wanted to let him go again.

When we finally separated to breathe, he pulled me into a hug and rested his forehead against mine. We stood there, breathing in and out as one, listening to the chirps of the crickets and the wind singing in the oak trees.

And in that moment, I knew I'd finally found my forever.

THE END

TWENTY

Epilogue

TWO AND A HALF YEARS LATER

J osie went bursting ahead of us into the front door of the Sweet Nothings Bake Shop, all energetic excitement, with Jensen and me trailing behind her. She looked back and forth, and spotted her Aunt Celia sitting with the Charitable Matrons of Adele.

They were having a disagreement of some kind, par for the course for those colorful ladies.

"I am telling you it would work!" a woman in a red hat with a purple feather argued. Mrs. Jones or Mrs. Hardt? I couldn't ever tell which of the twins it was.

"And I am telling you, no one is going to go for it!" Mrs. Lindy, a town legend, argued back just as vehemently.

"Well, we have to do something new, now, don't we? We can't just keep doing the same old fundraisers. We have a big goal this year, Merlene!" Dolly Blake interjected.

Mrs. Lindy huffed. "Yes, yes, I know. The preservation of the old firehouse is very important, but that doesn't mean the town's single ladies want to go on the auction block for it!"

My eyebrows shot up, and I looked over to Jensen. What were they cooking up now?

"Aren't you glad that no longer applies to you, whatever it is?" he whispered, leaning closer and wrapping a comforting arm around my expanding midsection.

"Absolutely." We'd been married a year ago, and I was six months along with our son now, so it *definitely* no longer applied to me. Thank heavens.

Josie waited patiently at my Aunt Celia's side for a break in the conversation, and I was proud of how she'd grown and changed over the last few years. She was still feisty and full of life and wonder, but she was slowly learning restraint as she grew. It made my mama's heart proud to see how she'd come through the bad times and retained all her sweetness. She was a good egg, my oldest.

Oldest felt surreal. I still couldn't believe how different things were now than when we'd first moved back to Adele three years ago. I was re-married to a man who was the complete opposite of my cheating ex, Josie was thriving, and a new bundle of joy was on the way. I'd never felt more loved, or more like I was right where I was meant to be.

"Well then, we're all waiting to hear what *your* brilliant idea is, Merlene."

Mrs. Lindy narrowed her eyes, and it was like she grew taller with indignation. Her cottony hair quivered as she leaned forward, a glint of mischief in her eyes. "I say, we flip it. Put the *men* on the block. Have a bachelor auction! The ladies can bring their pocket money and donate to a good cause in exchange for a date with a handsome man of their choosing." She locked eyes with Mrs. Purple Feather, daring her to argue.

She pursed her lips, thinking it over.

"Now *I'm* the one who's glad," Jensen whispered with glee.

Finally, Josie caught the lull she'd been waiting for. "Excuse me. Hi, Aunt Celia! We're here to pick up some croissants and coffee before we go crib shopping."

All the ladies tittered with glee and shifted their attention to my baby bump. I waved lightly, hoping they'd go back to their weird argument. The center of attention was my least favorite place to be. As if sensing my discomfort, Jensen gave me a little squeeze, and then waved as well.

"How are the loveliest ladies in Adele doing this fine afternoon? We're sorry to interrupt, it sounds like you've got some real important discussions happening here. But, you know how it is, we're excited to prepare for the little one."

He rested a gentle hand on my belly, and my heart melted into a puddle of goo, just like it did every night when he did the same thing before we went to sleep. Jensen had always been amazing with Josie, and he was proving so attentive now that I was pregnant, as well. I wanted for nothing, except maybe one less midnight trip to the bathroom.

Me and the nugget were still discussing that one.

"Of course you are!" Celia smiled wider than the Mississippi as she rose, gave us a quick embrace, then crossed to the counter to gather up our usual weekend order. She seemed happy to gain a moment's reprieve from the bluster at her table.

"I don't hate it, but so many of the town's bachelors have been married the last few years!" Mrs. Purple Feather squinted her eyes at Jensen, as if he was personally responsible for their lack of eligible men.

"Oh, there are still a few in town. Like your nephew—right, Dolly?"

Dolly froze up like a deer in a spotlight. "Well, yes, my Finn is still eligible," she said with a righteous sniff.

"See, there's our first bachelor. I know George will talk him into it, after he's found his sweet wife. And there are a few mamas around here who *want* their boys getting a move on, as we all know." Mrs. Lindy lifted her dainty teacup, a triumphant smile on her face.

"Don't forget the Fergusons, either. There are *five* of them not married. You know their mama wants a grandbaby *yesterday*, and can you blame her? Not a one married. Not *one*. You know Ruby will have them on our dating block in no time flat," Pearl chimed in from the end.

"Oh yes, and the Stockton boy!" someone else supplied.

"And Mark, my grandson!" Mrs. Bradenton chimed in.

I looked at Jensen wide-eyed and mouthed a silent "Woooow!" at him. There were going to be some grumpy fellows around town, and I wasn't too sure that was charitable of these ladies in the least. From the gleams in their eyes as they bandied the names of more men who were taking too long to settle down, they weren't going to give up this plan any time soon.

But, you know what they say: all's fair in love and small-town matchmaking.

Hey again, lovely reader! Thank you for spending your time reading Waiting on Forever. I truly hope you enjoyed it, and seeing the next chapter in the lives our friends in the tiny town of Adele. The next book follows Finn—Dolly's nephew—and his Bach-elor-Auction-match, Ivy. He's as unlikely a hero as they come, but I think you'll love the story!

You can pre-order The Bachelor Bargain here!

Before You Go . . .

Hey again, lovely reader! Thank you for spending your time reading Waiting on Forever. I truly hope you enjoyed it, and seeing the next chapter in the lives our friends in the tiny town of Adele. As of now, I've still got a few books in mind for this series, as well as something percolating for the Ferguson brothers. What do you think? Would you like to know more? Let me know! Your reviews help me decide whether a series is enjoyed, and should be continued.

Speaking of, if you would take a moment to leave a rating or review before you go on to your next read, I would be **so appreciative**! I'm still a new author, and every single review means a lot to me, as well as the other readers considering my books. So, thank you in advance—you're the best!

If you'd like to sign up for my mailing list so you never miss a new release, and get fun freebies from time to time like recipes, short stories, Advanced Review Copies, and more, you can do so here (su bscribepage.com/KristenDixon)!

I am available by email at kristendixonauthor@g mail.com as well, if you'd ever like to drop me a line directly!

Also By Kristen Dixon

Bless Your Heart (FREE!!!!!)
Thirty and unmarried in the south, can Marlie find
her forever wedding date? A romantic short story
sure to make you smile.

Bea Mine (Sweet Nothings Bake Shop, Book 1)
The quirky baker. Her best friend's off-limits older
brother. When sparks—and frosting—fly between
them, it'll be a Valentine's Day to remember.
When two stubborn southerners don't see eye to
eye, it's bound to cause sparks. But if these two can't

see heart to heart, it might just be the worst mistake the small town of Adele, Georgia has ever seen. This clean contemporary novella will have you falling in love from the first chapter.

Will Travel for Love (Sweet Nothings Bake Shop, Book 2)
A small town girl. An alluring British engineer who's just passing through. Will she follow her head, or lose her heart?
Check out book two of the Sweet Nothings Bake Shop series, and see what Celia's got up her sleeve for Daphne. Or should we say, who she's got up her sleeve?

Waiting on Forever (Sweet Nothings Bake Shop, Book 3)
She's healing from the blindside of divorce. He's a small-town hero. Can they build something together, or will it all fall apart?
With the two of them at odds, tension builds in the most unlikely of ways. Will her stubborn pride keep her lonely forever, or will Jensen be able to prove he's got enough heart to share with Maggie and her daughter?

The Bachelor Bargain (Sweet Nothings Bake Shop, Book 4)
An outspoken graphic designer. The town's most introverted bachelor. Will they open up to each other, or will the town's zany attempts at matchmaking push them further apart?
One sunset dinner won't change a thing . . . until it changes *everything*.

The Ferguson Brothers Series (coming 2023)

About the Author

Kristen Dixon was born and raised in Jacksonville, Florida, and is happily married with two kids. She has worked as a restaurant hostess, library book shelver, ranch hand, trail riding guide, and about twelve other unrelated fields, because variety—and sweet tea—is the spice of life. Not to mention a little thing called pursuing her passion of writing. She likes to write late in the evenings and thinks baking great cookies fuels hopes and dreams.

Her books are sweet, clean, and southern with real heart. If you like a classic southern gentleman, quirky side characters, and small towns, well, y'all came to the right place. Grab some tea, pull up a chair, and get ready to sit a spell.

If you would like to get all the latest news about her works, you can sign up for her newsletter at https://www.subscribepage.com/kristendixon and as always, don't forget to Follow on Amazon!